SEEKING
JUSTICE

SEEKING JUSTICE

By
Chris Hinch

Strategic Book Publishing and Rights Co.

Strategic Book Publishing and Rights Co.
12620 FM 1960, Suite A4-507
Houston, TX 77065
www.sbpra.com

ISBN: 978-1-62516-635-7

Book Design by Julius Kiskis

22 21 20 19 18 17 16 15 14   1 2 3 4 5

DEDICATION

Matthew Hinch, Margaret Jerome and finally Janet Cook without whose encouragement this book would never have been written.

Chapter 1

Oh God, can I make it? The sound of a bullet hitting the wall beside my head says I can. With the last of my strength, I pull myself over the fence, so tired I fall to the ground. I'm in a backyard. Over there are some steps. Going down, I find a door. Shit—it's locked. I hear footsteps and voices. How many are after me? I crouch down low in the darkest corner. It's a good thing black is my favourite color. I'm wearing a black leather jacket and black jeans. The voices are becoming clearer.

«Where is that fucker?»

«I heard a noise over here, so I took a shot. I didn't see anything, though.»

«You two look over there. Me and Frank will go this way.»

«What did this guy do to make you so pissed that you're after him like this? He's just a fucked up loser?»

«You heard about all the money that's missing? Well, he's the one who stole it!»

«No way, man. Couldn't be him. He's so stoned all the time he can't have a coherent thought in his head!»

«We'll talk later; we've got to get him now!»

Hearing their footsteps and voices fade, I become aware of my own fear. I am shaking, heart pounding, and I cannot catch my breath. Got to get away. I can't stand up. My arm

1

is all wet, and I'm sitting in a puddle. An unexpected pain doubles me over and almost makes me pass out. I'm what you call a crack head. I'm so out of shape, thin, and weak. If you saw me, you'd be amazed that I am still alive.

Wait a minute. How is this possible? Why did I run? Didn't I start all this so I could die with a clear conscience, make my life have some meaning?

I tried to kill myself before and failed—just like everything else I'd tried. All these months wasted, it is supposed to be over by now. Is there something inside of me that does not want me to die? Is there something there from before the drugs and self-defeat? Maybe I've found a new purpose, and that's what is keeping me holding on?

Where do I go from here? I'm too weak to run! Stay here and rest awhile. Let Frank and the others go away. Think of something that was real, lose myself in the past. Up until now, this insane situation could have been a stoned delusion. Something most drug users experience depending on the length of their addiction. The pain in my shoulder, though, tells me it is real!

I feel myself loosening up. Settling into the corner, my thoughts are going back to another me, one full of life, happiness, and laughter—the «me» before the drugs took complete control, my life before the lying, cheating, and stealing. A smile comes not just to my lips, but to all of me.

I feel a strange sensation in my arm and shoulder. The front and back of my shirt are soaked. All of a sudden a wave of pain hits me. God it hurts! I feel like passing out. Got to stay awake. Can't pass out now!

I have to concentrate on other things, not this mess I am in. I'm in bed. Jodie is asleep next to me. I reach for the mirror, do a couple of lines, and lie back feeling relaxed and excited. I crawl under the covers, start licking and kissing her legs. She tastes slightly salty and very exciting. I hear a moan of pleasure, and she starts to move onto her back. I start to kiss and lick my way up her body to reach her lips.

«Oh no, don't stop.» A pair of hands finds my head and pushes me back down. «Please don't stop!» I didn't!

Pure agony hits me, quickly replacing the pleasure! I run my hand up to my shoulder, feeling a hole in my jacket, wet and sticky. Oh fuck, not my jacket! It was the last thing Louisa gave me before she was taken out of my life. Tears fill my eyes; I can hardly see.

The door behind me suddenly pops open, and I fall inside the basement of the house. A little old lady stands over me. She opens her mouth to scream.

«Please help—somebody shot me,» I mutter in shock.

She brings me inside. I'm not much help—half dragged and crawling. I feel a hot, sticky mess on the floor. I did not realize that by leaning against the door, I was pushing it from the frame. Blood from the exit wound had run down the door into the basement.

«That's why I opened the door. I saw the blood. I'll get an ambulance,» the lady says calmly.

«Close the door, please,» I mutter, losing consciousness.

CHAPTER 2

I'm lying on a stretcher, things hooked up to my body—five or six things taped to my chest and two IV's in my arm. Doctors and nurses are standing all around me.

«You'll be okay now. We're taking you to surgery.» I feel a prick in my arm. «Count backwards to . . . «

I'm aware of lights and hear muffled voices, before passing out again. The pattern repeats itself a number of times before I finally can open my eyes. I have never felt so weak in my life. I cannot even lift my arm! Waves of fear hit me, and I pass out again. When I am finally among the living, there are two people in the room with me. One is obviously a doctor, dressed in his lab coat; and the other is my old school friend who became a «narc.» There are also two cops at the door.

«You gave us quite a scare. Almost lost you a few times. Don't worry, though. You'll be fine, just as soon as we fatten you up a bit,» the doctor says. «You're a lucky man! Your friend needs to talk with you, so I will see you in a while.»

My friend (I'll call him «Bob») looks at me, shakes his head, and says, «I thought you were a dead man. You just disappeared on me.»

«Sorry—I didn't have much choice. Did you find the camera?» I ask.

«No. Where is it?»

«On my AA medallion, the one on a pin, and the memory cards are in my NA fobs. I had a friend make them up for me. They should be in my things.»

Bob searches my bag of belongings, finds the items, and looks them over. «Wow, amazing things. I'll get the court attorney in here, and we'll get them into evidence. Hang on a bit,» Bob says, leaving the room. Within a few minutes he returns with a gorgeous blonde. They give me a receipt for the fobs and camera and put them into a baggie.

«We'll look these over and get back to you. Rest up, and don't worry, these guys won't let anything happen to you. See you soon!» Bob says, pointing to the two cops at the door. Bob and the blonde leave. Besides the two guards at the door, I'm alone.

The trouble with hospitals, besides the lousy food, is boredom. If you are a smoker and can't get out of bed, it's torture! There's too much time to think! The nurse tells me I weigh just over 100 lbs. Actually, it's 98 lbs., but I don't want to be called a «weakling.» I've been called too many names, and I don't want to add a new one! Liar, thief, lowlife, pond scum—you get the drift. It's funny how you remember the bad names and not the good. Maybe that's me. I never did feel good about myself. Guess it's time I sorted it all out. My life has been but hopefully won't be a mess anymore.

When I was younger, I wanted to be a cop. Things happen! I think the downhill slide began the day my brother stole my dad's rye and got me to drink it. I was thirteen. When Dad noticed the rye missing, my brother told him I took it. That was the only time my dad ever hit me, I didn't care because I felt so fucking good.

It was definitely downhill after that, slowly at first, then faster and faster. A friend got me smoking pot, and then I moved on to harder drugs. Guess where my ambition to be a cop went after that? My friend, «Bob,» did what I could not. He became a narc.

I went to a good school, in a really great neighbourhood—Kerrisdale, in Vancouver. A lot of my friends were rich, some were poor, but most were «middle of the road» like me. It was 1969, a time of sex, drugs, and rock and roll. All of my friends drank. Some did drugs, some sold them, and some even smuggled them. It was all very exciting, crazy, and sexy, but also dangerous. I don't know what turned me on most, the high, the sex, or the danger. Damn right—it was all of them!

I always had good dope, so it seemed people were always asking me to get it for them. At first, I mostly turned them down. I do not even know when that changed it was so gradual. I guess getting free drugs was the reason I eventually got it for other people. I didn't make money, just received free dope.

That's when I got into the cocaine. I always had jobs after I got a trade under my belt, until the blow. At first, I could not understand why I always had to get a new one. Nothing was as important as the cocaine.

I thought it was time to get married and settle down. That was a big mistake; that's when I found out I could not quit using. I had a car accident and could not walk unless I was stoned. It took the pain away. I snorted every day, all day and night. Sometimes I did some work for the guy I got it from, but mostly I sold it to support my habit. Both my wife and I were using, me much more than her. Things went from bad to worse, I started changing, getting weird thoughts, and having delusions. Eventually even my wife had had enough and told me to either, «Go to detox or get the hell out.»

I went to detox, where I found out how powerless I was

concerning cocaine. It was also where I first became aware
of the violence. While detoxing I had the shakes, could not
sit still, and wanted to leave so very badly. I stuck it out,
and after a few days I was feeling better. I was underweight,
but my appetite returned, and I ate and ate. I gained fifteen
pounds in ten days.

Some of the women I met in detox were all beat up.
Some had black eyes; one had a broken arm. They were
mostly prostitutes. Until then I had not been around that
kind of lifestyle, and it was an eye-opener. I was ashamed of
myself and angry with the people in the drug trade. I started
to think about turning people in for dealing. My friend Bob
came to my mind. I'm sorry to say that I did not do anything
about it, except to plan what to do if I ever did decide to do
something about it.

It did take five or six years to actually do something. A
very traumatic event finally triggered a response from me.
While at detox, my wife told me she wanted a divorce. I left
and got stoned. I stayed high for years, going into detox and
staying clean for a while, then out again.

I got a good paying job eventually and met a woman
who I thought did not do drugs. Boy was I wrong. People
might think it strange that a drug addict would not notice
somebody doing drugs. I didn't realize it for a long time.
I had been going to Narcotics Anonymous and Alcoholics
Anonymous meetings regularly, and it was finally getting
easier to not get high. One day I came home early and found
my girlfriend snorting coke. It really did bad things to my
head. Of course, I started to use again.

Life seemed so perfect. I had money coming in, living
with a woman I loved, getting high and actually enjoying it.
We'd have friends over, and we'd all get high, and when the

company left, we went to the bedroom for the greatest sex ever. Then things started to change for the worse.

«Are you going to work today?» she asked.

«Yeah, I'll give you a ride.»

After a cup of coffee we'd get into the car, and I dropped her at her work. On the way to my job I saw a guy I knew. I wasn't on my way to work anymore. «Do you have any blow?»

«Yeah,» I said, «at home.» Today was Friday, but something like that had happened every day that week. We got to my house, and I asked him if he had any money?

«$250. Today was payday,» he said.

«Okay, hand it over.» Going inside, I threw him an eight ball.

He grabbed a mirror, but I said, «No, I gotta go to work.»

«Aw come on. Janey will shit if I do this at home. I'll share it with you.» I could not turn it down.

It was a long time since I'd been able to turn anything down. Why did I bother getting a new job when I just kept losing them? Trying to fool myself, I guess. This time I had missed four out of five days at work. The truth was I could make more selling dope. I was thirty-four.

My friends were always hanging around wanting me to get them coke. My brother knew a lot of people who smuggled it in. Over the years I had gotten to know them all. It was as if my fate was sealed before I realized it was happening. My friends turned into customers. I'd get them drugs, they would do it at my house, and I would get high for free.

Funny how my life went—becoming a dealer was not what I had wanted or planned. Two or three hours would go by, three more people would show up, now it would be a party. I would tell them they all had to get out by 4:30 when

Jodie got home. There is coke in front of everybody, all of a sudden my door was kicked in. I thought, oh no, the cops; but my friend Mike said, «Oh no, it's Frank, and I know why he is here!" »

Chapter 3

I'm in a hospital bed, heart racing from the memory of that door crashing open. Gradually I calm down, but not before the nurse comes running in. «You okay?»

«Yeah, just remembering some things, I guess.»

«Well, you've got to take it easy. The heart monitor started beeping, and you are still very weak, so stay calm and relaxed,» she gently scolds.

As she's leaving, Bob shows up. «How's it going?»

I shrug my shoulders.

«We saw the video. We thought he was after you because of the people getting busted. But no, he thought you were stealing from him. On the video we saw someone we'll call 'Bill' come up to you and shoots. You go down, and Bill walks out of sight.

«'Frank, finish him off,'» someone says. Frank comes up to you and checks your pulse. «'Fuck,' he says angrily and goes running out the same way that Bill went.»

Bob continues to explain the footage. «We see you get up and stagger out the door holding your shoulder. The camera bounces around for a couple of blocks and then goes dead—just as you jumped over the gate, I think. Guess you jarred the battery loose or something.

«When we got to the house to bring you in, you were gone, and we saw all the blood. They think you stole their money,

10

not got people busted. We're still on if you want to keep going. What you're doing is a very good thing!» Bob adds.

«Did you grab the memory card from the camera I planted in the living room?» I ask Bob.

«No, we'll get it and see if it shows more than your camera does.»

«Good, do that. If it does, we can keep mine out of it for now. We'll talk more when you get it. It's in the electrical outlet near the door,» I explain as Bob heads out the door.

I always carried a camera on me, at all times. Over the past year or so I'd been planting them in various places. Depending on what the other camera picked up, I might not have to use my video to charge Bill. That would help keep who I was and what I was doing a secret.

Actually, Bill was only one of several people I wanted to get, but because I was doing so much coke (and was so out of control) going any further had seemed beyond my grasp. Now, after being in the hospital and away from the drugs, I am gaining strength, and very clearly it seems possible to keep on going. In addition, my newfound desire to live seems well worth exploring. I know a lot will depend on what the other camera shows. I cannot remember exactly where it was pointing because I was so close to death at that point. I nod off to sleep.

«It's almost time to get those assholes,» Bob announces as he bursts back into the room. «Your video shows pretty much the same thing, but you are in the picture this time.»

«Good, then we'll use that, instead of the one I was carrying. But don't arrest him yet, okay!»

«You're sure?»

«Yeah, I want to fix this mess with Frank before you go after Bill,» I explain.

«Okay, we'll do it your way for now.»

«Thanks. See you later. I need to rest.»

«Ok, take it easy!»

I want Bill killed, not arrested. But I have to do it in a way that looks like I'm not really involved. I can't do that if he is in jail. If Bill is the one who blamed me for the missing money, maybe I can turn it back on him. Bill and I don't like each other. Actually, I hate his fucking guts. He's one of the main reasons I'm doing this whole thing. Payback is going to be a bitch. Gotta get stronger so I can do it! Louisa was taken from me by these assholes, and they're all going to pay—Bill, Art, and anybody else I find.

Thinking of Louisa makes me feel like running away again, going to get loaded; but being this weak and having the two cops at the door stops that desire from being an option.

Gotta stay strong. My sanity is at risk again. Have to think of other things. The plans we were making. I had a bright future ahead. Then I met Frank! If only I had gone to work that day.

Lying there with nothing to do, thinking was not hard. In the past, drugs held the memories at bay. I used to be quite athletic, interested in all kinds of sports, soccer, baseball, kickboxing, boxing, and a few lessons in karate. Drugs took that away from me. Over the years, I needed all of those skills to keep some idiot away from me and my drugs.

I am 5'8'' tall and had recently been told Tom Cruise was lucky enough to look like me. To look at me now you would not believe I could even walk. I always had a girlfriend. I don't know why. I was always shy around girls.

This thinking about me, in an unemotional way, was new to me, but my memories of Louisa were always there to haunt me.

CHAPTER 4

I still remember the surprise and yes, more than a little fear, when that door came crashing open.

«Sorry, but your asshole friend there owes me money,» Frank says to me, while pointing at Mike.

«Guess that's between you and him, and you'll have to pay for the door!»

«Guess not. Mike says you owe him money, and I think that's my coke you're snorting.»

«No, it's my dope, and I owe Mike nothing! Actually, he owes me.»

Mike is trying to hide in the corner of the couch. He's not doing a very good job of it.

«Well, what's going on here, Mike, and why does he say I owe him money?» I ask. Mike ignores me, looking at the mirror that his coke is on. Clearly he wants to have some.

«We let him come over here to collect the money you owe him,» Frank explains. «He said he fronted you three ounces.»

«No. In fact, I just fronted him a gram,» I correct Frank.

«Let me try some of that, and I'll know if it's mine.» Frank bends, snorts a line, waits a bit and says, «Hey, that's better than mine. Sorry about this. We'll take this outside and leave you out of it,» Frank nods. He throws me a one hundred dollar bill. «That's for the door and the line,» he says. Mike and Frank leave.

That's the thing with coke. Mike comes over here nervous and heading for the back door. I offer him a line. He walks over to me and does it. A few minutes later he asks if I would front him some. I hand him a gram. He sits down and does some more. He forgets the reason he came here and remembers only when the door is kicked open. Nothing is as important as the next line.

About twenty minutes go by, and I hear something at the door. Mike is there with two black eyes, missing a few teeth, and a broken arm. He's covered in blood. It's pouring out of his nose and mouth. I bring him inside and blood gets everywhere—on the sofa, the coffee table, and the white rug—what a mess. I call an ambulance, clean up the coke, and put the pipes and mirrors away.

The police arrive first. Neighbours saw Mike on the sidewalk coming into my place and phoned them. A minute later the ambulance shows up. My place is small. My friends are there, as well as two cops and two ambulance attendants. They cannot help but step in the blood, tracking it all over the place. One of the cops looks familiar. I think it dawns on us both at the same time. We both know Bob, the chief of the narcotics division. I was uptight before, but now I feel worse because my friend will hear about it. That's when Jodie walks in, sees all the mess, and freaks out. What a fuckin' day this is.

That day she walks out of my life. Frank steps in. A couple of days later I'm at home, having lost another job and going to have to move. I'm feeling pretty down when Bob shows up at the door.

«Man, I'm worried about you. I thought you had gone to detox and were going to meetings!»

«Yeah I was, but, you know, things happen.»

«Well, the cop who was here the other day told me about what happened here. The people you're involved with are not the kind you want to stay involved with. We have been watching them both for a while now. Mike is pretty stupid. We'll give him some rope, and he will hang himself. Frank, on the other hand, is pretty smart. We can't get anything on him. The only reason we know about him is because Mike sees him a lot. They seem to be old friends.»

Bob and I go way back. Hell, we lost our virginity on the same night to the same girl. We went to a party, and on the way in I see this good-looking girl. Our eyes meet, lock together, and somehow we end up in someone's bed. We were fooling around for what seemed like forever.

We end up naked and she says, «Can you hold it? I don't want to get pregnant.»

«Sure,» I say, but I was getting off at the same time I was going in. She leaves, feeling more than a little unsatisfied, and I see her latch on to Bob just to piss me off. They brush past me. I wink at Bob, give him a high sign. They come out, Bob all smiles and red in the face, the girl still looking unsatisfied. She should not have picked on two virgins.

Anyway, we had some great times together. We had both gone to the same school, played soccer, baseball, pool, did everything together. We were both going to be cops.

Bob says, «You gotta clean up your act again, or you're gonna end up in jail.»

«Yeah, I know. It just seems to take over, you know. It's hard to quit. The hold it has is so powerful,» I say in a matter of fact way.

«If you want to talk, I will always find the time,» Bob says.

An hour or so after Bob leaves there is a knock on my door. It's Frank, waving a few flaps of coke in my face. How could I say no? As we're doing the first few lines, Frank starts telling me about Mike. I had bought from Mike a few times.

«Me and my friends front Mike a lot of the time. He fucks up now and again, but he has always pulled through in the end. Your name comes up often. He says he fronts to you all the time, and it takes you awhile to pay him back,» Frank informs me.

«I never front from him; his blow is not that good. He cuts it, and I don't trust him. He gets coke from me, but I always make him pay cash,» I explain to Frank. When Frank's blow is all gone, I bring out some of mine. He is really impressed by it.

«Man, this is good, way better than mine. Do you have a few ounces?»

«Yeah, you want some?» I ask.

«Yeah. I'll go out to the car for the money, be right back.» Frank makes me nervous. He just had this intensity about him. What Bob had to say about him also makes me nervous.

Frank comes back, and I give him most of my stash, saying, «I'd give you more, but the rest is personal.»

«That's okay for now, but can you get more?»

«Sure, every day. It's always there,» I tell him.

«Okay. I have to show this to some people.»

«Was there more you were going to tell me about Mike?» I ask.

«Yeah. He has been telling people that you are fucking up, and you owe him lots of money.»

«I guess he's blaming me for his problem. You should cut him off,» I tell Frank. «I owe him nothing!»

«Well, he has been putting us off for over a week. He told us he had fronted it to you. We were waiting out front in the car for him.»

«Yeah, he was pretty nervous when he got here, but he did some lines, calmed down, and then you came in.»

«Well, we were going to beat the shit out of you. I tried your blow, and I knew Mike had lied to us,» Frank explains.

«I was wondering why you came in. This is a bit scary. You know my girlfriend left me because of all this, and my landlord gave me an eviction notice. Mike—what a cocksucker.»

«Isn't he, though?» Frank agrees.

«He won't be coming around here anymore. If he tells you I owe him money again, you'll know he's lying!»

«Okay, I'll know. I'm going to send a friend over to visit. Save some of that for her, okay?»

«Sure.» I nod at him.

«I have to go. See ya soon.»

Half an hour later there is a knock on the door. I open it, and there is a gorgeous girl standing there, maybe twenty-two or twenty-three years old.

«Frank said to come over and cheer you up.» She hands me the ounces I sold to Frank and says, «I'm not leaving till it's gone!» She cheered me up too. Kept it up, and up, and up, until the coke was all gone.

I did not know for a while why Frank was being so nice to me. I thought it was because he was feeling guilty. Later he told me he was having problems with his supplier and was looking for new sources.

«I don't want to be the middleman very often. I want to stay small time, just make a bit of money and get high,» I tell Frank.

«Okay. Can you ask your friend if I can meet him? I'll give you something every time we do a deal.»

«Sounds good to me,» I say, liking the idea.

    I introduced Frank to him the next day. From then on every four or five weeks my gorgeous little friend would deliver an ounce of coke, and she would stay until it was all gone. She was a habit I fully enjoyed.

Chapter 5

God I'm tired of lying here. Maybe it's time to get out of bed. I've been lying here for three days. I sit up, feeling a little dizzy. I stay sitting that way for a few minutes until I feel better. Swinging my legs over the side of the bed, I almost pass out. Slowly the faintness goes away. I roll over on my stomach as I start to slide to the floor, stopping myself just in time. I get my legs under me, holding on to the bed with all my strength. I've never felt so weak in my life.

It takes a long time before I can finally stand on my own. My legs feel tingly and numb at the same time. Still holding onto the bed, I make my way around it and slowly work my way back, sweat dripping from my forehead. God help me. This is hard.

I hear somebody clearing his throat. I turn, and Bob is standing near the door.

«How long have you been there?» I ask, turning red in the face.

«I watched you sit up and get out of bed and walk around it. You think you should be up and about?» he asks with concern.

«I've got to get stronger, lots to do!»

«That's why I'm here. To see what we should do. You know you've got to take it easy. You're still pretty fucked up. The doctor says your blood pressure is way up, and you are a walking skeleton,» Bob lectures.

«Sure, sure, just so bored and so weak it's scary. If someone came after me now, I'd be pretty helpless!» I confess.

«Don't worry. Those two guys outside the door won't let anybody in.»

«I've been thinking about how to get Frank on my side again. We have to make him believe Bill is the one ripping him off, which is probably the truth,» I suggest.

«We put out a warrant on him for attempted murder, but he is nowhere to be found.»

«Guess that's that, then,» I sigh. I feel happy about this information. I need him out of jail where I can get to him.

«Yup,» Bob says, not suspecting what I was really feeling.

«So where are we on all the other stuff?» I ask.

«We arrested a lot a lot of people all the way up to Frank. It would be nice to get the ones above him,» Bob says with feeling.

«That's what I've been lying here thinking about. It all hinges on getting Frank's trust back. I guess we'll have to pick up Bill and go from there. Let's hold off on the drug busts until you get Bill. I'll think of something because I really want these guys. On second thought maybe pick up some of the ones that you can. Don't use my information to get them if you can avoid it.»

«Yeah, that way they will have to bring in some new blood, shake them up some,» Bob agrees. «Got to get going. See you when we round some of them up.»

I lie there with questions racing through my brain. Can I somehow get to Frank before they get Bill? If I do, maybe Frank and his friends will take care of him for me. This is what I want, what I need, and what I will have.

How to get out of here? I'll have to be stronger, able to move around a bit without falling on the floor. For the rest of the day and most of the next I practise walking. I make very good progress. I come up with my plan of escape as well.

In an hour or so I'm scheduled for a check-up in a room down the hallway. That room has a connecting door to another cubicle. My two guards will stay in the hallway between the rooms. Hopefully, I can go in one room, get dressed, and go out the other door. One thing I know I can count on. You always have to wait for a doctor or nurse to get there when you go for a visit. The cops will be looking for people going in but not coming out. Once out of the hospital there is a good chance I might not be able to come back.

Hopefully, Frank will at least talk to me before he gets rid of me. I've always found that if you go face someone in person you are more than halfway believed already. It takes guts to do this, but then I really have no other choice. Am I trying to get killed again, or do I honestly think this is the only way?

Let's just do this, no more thinking. I put my clothes under me in the wheelchair and wait a few more minutes for the orderly. He comes, we go to the room, and I get dressed. Even that is almost too much for me. I rest a few minutes, open the door, and walk the few yards to the elevator. It feels like an eternity until it arrives, and with great relief I step in.

Soon I am in a cab and on my way to Frank's. It's a half-hour drive, giving me a little time to rest. I know if he is there he will be alone. Frank has split up with his wife, and he never lets his business come into his home.

Lately, when alone and bored, I start thinking about the past. Fortunately, I have been able to do so without going out and getting loaded. Not so in the past.

I was at Ed's house to collect some money he owed me.

Bill comes in with his girlfriend. We're sitting there, and Ed asks Bill's girlfriend if she has his money. Bill freaks.

«Why do you owe him money?»

«She fronted an eight ball and has not paid me back yet,» Ed explains.

Bill gets up and starts beating her, punches her in the face and kicks her. I get up and hit him over the head with a frying pan. I kick him out of Ed's, telling him not to come back. People who beat on women send me to a crazy place. That's the reason Bill hates me.

I hate him for entirely another reason, but I can't think about that yet. I don't know if I am strong enough to deal with the memory. I also have to keep a clear head if I am to deal with Frank.

CHAPTER 6

After thinking about Bill, my anger is almost out of control. This is probably a good thing. I'll be able to deal with Frank with no show of fear.

The only way I will be able to convince Frank I was not responsible is to be upfront and honest. I am almost positive it was Bill who was the thief. He is such a fucking asshole. I've been to Bill's house a few times and planted cameras and mikes in various rooms. I have watched some of the video. It showed him smoking crack all day and night. He was very paranoid after a few hits. He would wander around his apartment carrying knives and a few times had a gun. I would be afraid to drop in on him unexpectedly. He has to be spending a lot of money to do as many drugs as he is doing.

How do I get Frank to listen to me?

The cab stops in front of Frank's house, and I ask the driver to pull up as far as he can. Even with the anger, I'm still pretty shaky. I pay the driver, get out, and walk to the door with no hesitation.

Frank is watching out the window, a look of astonishment on his face. He opens the door saying, «What the fuck are you doing here?»

«I want some fucking answers! What was that all about?»

«You've been stealing from us, after all I've done for you,» Frank yells back.

«What do you mean—what you've done for me? I'm the one that's been keeping you in business for fuck sake.»

«People tell me you've been spending a lot of money lately. Not a word about where it came from. I never told Bill to shoot you. He did that on his own.»

«Let me guess—Bill is the one who told you that it must be me,» I hiss back at him.

Frank looks at me, and I can almost see the thoughts racing through his mind. «What were you doing at the stash anyway?» he asks.

«I called Bill looking for you, and he told me that was where you were going to be. He did not say it was your stash house. I had no way of knowing it was,» I reply in an offhand way.

«The money was missing from there. I walk in, and there you were,» Frank tries to explain.

«Why would I go there if I'd taken the money?» I say with sincerity. I can tell he believes me more and more. «You think I would show up at your house if I was hiding something?»

«No,» he says, a guilty look on his face.

«Ask people about Bill. He's been doing a lot of base lately. How is he paying for it?» I continue very reasonably.

«Okay. You stay here, and I'll make some phone calls.»

As he goes out, he says, «There's a Pepsi in the fridge. Help yourself.»

I grab a pop, sit down, and realize I'm sweating. Exhaustion or fear—guess it does not matter which. I'm bleeding again and get very drowsy. It's hard to keep my eyes open—.

Somebody is shaking me! «Wake up. I talked to some people, and they tell me the same story. Bill is acting

strangely and looking over his shoulder a lot, very jumpy,»
Frank says, sitting down in a chair. «I didn't want to think
it was you. We've always been straight with each other. Bill
was very convincing when he was telling me he thought it
was you.» Frank sounded apologetic.

«Well, he has to blame someone. Ever since I hit him,
he's hated my guts!» I grin.

«Yeah, I forgot about that.» Also with a big grin.

He looks at me closely. «It took a lot of guts to come
here,» with admiration in his voice.

«How much choice did I have? It was either do this or get
out of town. I don't have the money for that!» I grin again.

«Well, we're going to set Bill up. See if he takes the bait.
I believe you, but the other guys want proof. Don't worry. I
didn't tell them you were here,» he says with an earnest look.

«Thanks.»

«Man, you look dead on your feet. You okay?»

«No.» I look at my arm, and it's still bleeding. «Fuck,
got to go get this looked at. When are you going to set Bill
up?» I ask.

«Tomorrow or the next day,» he answers with a little smile.

«I've got to go back to the hospital. You trust me enough
to let me do that?» I ask him.

«Yeah, I already called a cab to get you out of here.
I thought some of the guys might want to come over and
discuss this. I don't want you here if they do.»

«Okay, I'll be at St. Paul's Hospital. They let me out
of ICU yesterday. Think I'll be back in there again. You're
going to owe me big time for this, Frank.»

«Yeah, yeah, I know!» he says with guilt in his voice.

The cab pulls up. Frank helps me in, tells the driver, «St. Paul's
emergency, hurry!» I stay awake for about half the journey.

Late the next day I become conscious back in ICU, weaker than before, but not nearly so worried, and thinking, Revenge is gonna be oh so sweet!

All the bullshit with Bill and Frank has brought up all the anguish again, about Louisa being killed. We'd been out to a restaurant. Just about to cross the street, I remember my coat.

«Be right back. Meet you at the car,» I tell her. I run inside, grab my coat, and come back outside. I hear a squeal of tires and a thump. I see taillights going up the street away from me. I don't see Louisa at our car. I look around and see something in the street about fifty yards away. At first, I think it's nothing since it's so far away.

Where's Louisa? She should be right here! I was only gone a minute. I walk up the street towards the lump on the ground. As I get closer, I make out the clothes Louisa was wearing. Oh, God no! I run up, and it's her, lying in a growing pool of blood. She's not breathing; her arms and legs are at funny angles.

I don't know CPR. What do I do? I get out my cell phone and call 911. When the ambulance arrives, I'm sitting in the middle of the road with Louisa's head in my lap. They make me move and start checking her out. They look at each other, and one of them shakes his head.

«Fuck,» one of them says so softly I can barely hear. They look at me and notice all the blood on me. «You okay, bud?»

I cannot answer. My brain is not working right. All I see is my life, dead on the ground. The ambulance guys check me out, and I think I hear them say the blood is not mine. I don't remember much more of that night except the emptiness inside. I wanted to die, and for the next four years I did everything in my power to do so. I was high all the time. I even got into heroin. Some asshole sold some to me mixed with coke. My brother was a junkie for thirty years, but he's another part of this story, later.

Louisa and I had been out celebrating. She had just found out she was pregnant. I could not understand what happened, why she had died. She had not had a drink all night because of the baby growing inside of her. I'd been going to AA meetings and had just had my three-year cake. Life was good. When Louisa died, I fell apart again.

My life has been like that—a vicious circle, clean and sober for awhile, fucked up for awhile, detox, clean and sober for awhile, fucked up—around and around in an endless circle.

After Louisa died, I sold a lot of drugs, not caring if I got busted or not, died or not. Nothing mattered. Frank would let me get fucked up only to a point; then he would make me go to detox. I would go in weak and fragile. With a little of the weight I had lost back on, I was strong enough to start all over. Never able to regain all the weight I had lost over the years, I got really skinny and weak. The reason I went to detox was so I could get strong enough to stay high.

Got to stop these memories. They're taking me to places I don't want to go. I've been remembering all the people who are no longer living. Drugs are the main reason they're dead. There were overdoses, suicides, and even murder. It started at school. I can think of about ten people who died there. Not all of them were friends, but we went to the same parties. Not to mention the living dead, the ones with no help, no hope, and no human decency left to them.

During that time, a couple years after Louisa died, I was getting really angry with the drug dealers, myself included. I wanted to get them all off the street, in jail, or even dead. I was so wasted and paranoid there was no way I could pull it off.

My shoulder is really starting to hurt. I look for the call bell. I want to get some of those pain meds. Man, gotta stop wanting to get high.

The orderly comes by with dinner. I'm just starting to eat when Bob comes in. He has pizza, my favourite—ham and pineapple.

«Where the fuck did you get to? When did you start bleeding again?»

«Had to go see Frank, and I think I convinced him it was not me. He let me leave, even called the cab.»

«You got the two officers in a lot of shit. You'd better make it up to them,» Bob lectures, waving his finger.

«Okay, I will. What do you think this is all about anyway? It's not about me. I need to find out who killed Louisa. I told Frank where I am. Maybe he'll come. I'll know everything is okay then, that he believed what I told him.»

«Okay, I'll tell the officers to let him in if he comes by. They know what he looks like. They'll search him when he comes in, though.» He looks at me with concern written all over his face. «Don't you ever do that again. You're too good a guy to get yourself killed now.»

«I know, but it had to be done. I want to continue this, and I'm beginning to feel that it's not over for me yet,» I say, hope in my voice.

«That's great, but we still have to sort some things out.»

«Have you picked anyone up yet?» I ask.

«About seven people, maybe a couple more since I've been here,» Bob says.

«That will make some of the bosses make an appearance. Keep an eye out for them.»

«Yeah, I will. I'd better go. Frank might come by anytime; if he sees me, it will be difficult for you.» As Bob gets to the door he says, «Smarten up, and take care of yourself. This room is yours for a lot longer now. It will be easier to watch you.»

«Yeah, see you.» I wave. I've been lying here with nothing to do except think about things, Frank for one. I kind of liked Frank. It's the people I met through him that I didn't like. Frank is a middleman, sets the deals up. Frank does blow, but for him it is not a problem. He can say no to it. He is not violent, and he knows how to have a good time. He is generous, at least to me. What can I say? We get along! I have not wired Frank's house and do not say or do much against him. If I do find out anything different, he's going to be gone, also.

Frank arrives in my room about an hour after Bob has left. He is searched and let in.

«Man, you look awful,» are his first words.

«Thanks.»

«The guys were talking about the stash house where Bill could hear them. They could see he was really stoned, very jumpy. He'd been beat up, had black eyes, and was limping. His whole attitude changed after he heard that it was the same house.

«When Bill left to go home we followed him, and sure enough that's where he went. We came in just as he was putting the money into his pockets. The guys beat him up some more. I tried to stop them, but they would not listen. I told them to let it go; don't have any more to do with him. It's the normal way, get beat up for stealing, be cut off, no more dope. I left and came over here. Looks like you're in the clear.»

«You're sure?» I ask.

«Not a problem, they know it wasn't you.»

«Okay, what do we do now?» I say.

«Well, we gotta get you back on your feet and off the dope for good, fatten you up. Get that girl of yours to keep you happy.»

«I've been thinking that myself, but I didn't want her to see me like this!»

«I'll go see her, get her to come around here,» Frank offers.

«Thanks,» I say gratefully. «Don't worry. I'll make it up to you somehow.»

«I owe you for what's happened. Don't worry about it,» Frank says. I already feel a lot better about the whole thing.

«You're sure it's gonna be okay?» I ask.

«Positive. Okay, I have to go now, but I'll be back.»

Chapter 7

Bob comes in a while later carrying my laptop.

«Wow man, thanks. Now I can watch some movies, maybe get on the Internet.»

«Got something to show you.» he plugs in the laptop. After it boots up, I see Frank and three other guys coming up behind Bill. He's putting something in his pocket. It's obvious that he's already been beaten very badly. The three guys start to kick the shit out of him some more. Frank is yelling at them to stop. They push him away and tell him to leave.

«Let him go. Just don't have anything more to do with him,» Frank yells.

«Don't worry. We've got it handled. Get out of here.»

Frank leaves. One of the guys checks to see if Frank is gone. He comes back and says, «Yeah. I saw him get in his car and drive away.»

The three men stand around Bill, who is whimpering and begging them to stop. «Are you the one who took the money from here before?» one of them asks, grabbing him by the throat. He lets go so Bill can answer.

«Yeah, it was me, not Chris. I'll pay it back I promise. I got so fucked up on the blow, couldn't help myself.»

«Well, you're going to pay. Give me the money you just took.»

Bill hands the money to one of the men. Two seconds

31

later one of the men standing behind him reaches around and slits his throat. Blood sprays and then gushes everywhere.

«You stupid son of a bitch, you've got blood all over us. Clean this mess up and get rid of him,» one of them yells at the killer. They go to a closet, pull clean clothes off some hangers, and get changed. The man who cut Bill's throat is busy rolling him up in a tarp and cleans up the blood.

Bob stops the video.

«We'd been watching the house and heard the sounds of a fight. Then we saw Frank leave. We saw another guy look out the window and watch Frank drive off. A few minutes later, two of the men, dressed in different clothes than before, get in a car and drive away. About half an hour later the third man brings out a box and tries to get it in his car. He's having a tough time so I go over to him and ask if he needs help. I have my cop friend with me. He's in uniform. The guy freaks and tries to get away.

«That's when we found Bill inside the box. We went into the house to see if your camera had caught all this.» Bob pauses. «This video clearly shows that you and Frank are off the hook. Bill told them you did not steal from them. We also have proof that Frank did not murder Bill. I think you are going to be left alone now,» he adds.

I watch the video a couple of more times and then delete it. I don't need anyone finding it on my computer. The way Bill's blood came pumping out of him was fascinating but very creepy. I did not know how I felt about it. Glad he was gone, glad Frank was not part of it, and very glad no one knew the part I played in it.

I read a lot, mostly detective thrillers and some spy novels. I hate it when the author is stuck for a way to keep the action going and just puts in some stupidity. The good guy is after a psycho killer who not only kills his victim but the whole family. The psycho finds out the good guy is after him, so he goes after our hero and his family. Funny how the hero never stops to protect the ones he loves. The only one he saves is himself. He just goes to work with not a care in the world. Next thing you know, his family are all dead. I almost have to stop reading a book like that.

One of the main reasons it has taken me so long to go after the dealers in my world is the people I love. With the death of Louisa, I have nobody, no friends, just customers. I have no one to be careful about, except maybe Frank. He knows what business he's in and will just have to take his chances. I was not even in the equation, not worth saving.

The nurse comes in and rearranges my bed. She's not overly gentle, accidently bumps my shoulder.

«Hey, watch what you're doing.» I put my hand up and feel the bandage and the wetness. «I know you. Aren't you Sue's sister?» Sue and I used to get loaded together, but I had not seen her around lately. A lot more wreckage I have to live with.

She glares at me and says, «Asshole.»

I don't swear at women. I swear quite a lot but rarely at other people. I reach for my wallet, take out ten dollars and hold it out to her.

She's about to take it and asks, «What's this for?»

«Oh, to help with your problem,» I say angrily.

«What problem?» she asks me.

«They say Vagisil really helps. Now get out of here.»

I call one of the cops standing guard at the door. «Don't let her in again. She did this,» I say almost shouting, pointing at my arm, which is bleeding again. I buzz for the nurse, who has to change my bandages. Luckily no stitches are broken.

My new girlfriend, Margaret, comes in. She takes one look at me, and her face turns as pale as mine. «What happened to you?»

I gather that Frank did not tell her everything, wanting me to explain. He's left it up to me to tell her what his involvement was. Since she is part of this great plan of mine, it does not take me long to fill her in.

Margaret lies next to me on the bed, looking at the bulge under the covers. «That better not be a gun,» she says playfully. She puts her hand under the covers. «We'll have to make sure it doesn't go off too soon.»

The gasp I make brings in one of the cops, who looks down and sees what's going on. «I won't let anybody in.» He winks and walks out.

One thing I love about Margaret—she spoils me rotten, does whatever I want. Sliding under the covers, she takes me into her mouth. I was afraid the cops out front would come in again with the noises I was making.

CHAPTER 8

Margaret was the girl that kept coming by with the ounces of coke. She would not leave until it was all gone. She is Franks' relative by marriage, a niece I think. She also knows Mike and had previously met me once or twice.

Margaret liked me and wanted to get to know me better. When she heard Frank ask another girl to bring the ounces back to me, she asked if she could deliver it. We did not get serious about each other for a long time, keeping it playful and private. She was very beautiful and sexy, and she liked the same sort of sex I did. Amazing what can happen in a hospital. I fall asleep wishing for a cigarette. Margaret is gone when I wake up. «Back after work,» the note reads.

I've been planting cameras for a long time now and giving the memory cards to Bob. Since I am a drug addict and not a cop, I don't know about the law. I don't know and don't care. I just go in and plant the cameras. They have audio and video, and the quality is excellent. I don't need to worry about warrants, wiretaps, or any other type of warrant. I am simply a concerned citizen.

I also have a friend who sells surveillance equipment, cameras in teddy bears called Nanny Cams, phone recorders—all the stuff you see on TV and in the movies. I had been doing this sort of thing a long time before Bob came into it all. My friend has two stores that I know about. He calls them spy stores. He also helps me install some of them. He is an ex-coke freak who got into the business because of the paranoia you get from regular cocaine abuse.

The agreement is for Bob and his boys to try and get other evidence so they do not have to use my videos in court. That way I can continue what I am doing and remain safe. I don't know all the legal details; all I know is that my name is to be left out as long as possible. Most of the people I have given him so far are not important, but there are a few he's arrested who really needed to be in jail.

I've been trying with a lot of success to meet new dealers big and small. One day I was introduced to a guy after I had bought his drugs from a «friend.» His dope was good, so I asked to meet him. After I bought from him a few times, he gave me a flap of heroin mixed with coke. Thinking it was just blow, I took a really big hit. I started to get dizzy, my head spinning. I made it outside and passed out in a snow bank. I would have died except for a woman passing by. After a few minutes she was able to get me up. It really pissed me off. I started watching him carefully after that, catching on camera everything he did.

A young girl, who looked fifteen or sixteen, owed him some money. He raped her while she was unconscious. The camera I planted in his house caught it all. I had been delayed in getting the memory card for a few weeks. He did not leave his apartment, and the delay caused the girl a lot of extra pain. He slapped her around and then made her go and work the streets.

She had been buying blow from him at first. Then he switched it to coke mixed with heroin. She was, as he put it, «his property» and «had to do» as he said. All this was recorded on camera, safely in my computer and on a memory card. He was one of the first I helped to get arrested. I tuned him up a little before the police arrived. Another reason I was glad I was not a cop. I could beat him up a little and get away with it. I made up my mind right then. There was more I wanted to find out about him.

Helping to nail pricks like that made me feel as if I was paying back some of the bad I had done. It also showed Bob that what I was doing was very important.

The girl had been doing drugs since she was twelve, in and out of foster care, about four or five years. How do you reach someone as young and screwed up as her? She was put in social services' care. They put her in the hospital, cleaned her up. Hopefully that will be the last I see or hear of her for quite a while. Hope she does okay.

The police guard at my door is gone. Everybody seems to feel the danger is over. I think it might be just beginning again. There's an undercover cop working as an orderly. He's there «just in case.» Frank comes into the room with a guy I have not met before. He is introduced as «Ken.»

«We came by to assure you that you don't have to worry about anything,» Ken begins. «When you are strong enough and can stay off the drugs, there are some things you can do with us. It will help pay for what was done to you. You'll meet some new people and be able to make some good money. Frank tells me you've been pretty fucked up over the death of your wife. You seem to be getting over it. I hope so,» he says, looking me straight in the eye.

«Sounds good to me, can always use some extra money.»

«You've got a good friend here,» Ken says, pointing to Frank. Frank lowers his head when he hears this, gets red in the face.

«Well, we'll see you when you get out. Rest up, and stay

clean,» Frank says.

The doctors are worried about how much blood I lost. They inform me there is a risk of brain damage, as well as damage to the nerves. I gather I could have been a mental midget as well as crippled. Loss of blood also means loss of oxygen to your body and brain. My brain seems okay to me, but others might think it was damaged. Why else would I want to keep doing this? At least that's how I think I must appear to them. I seem to walk okay except for feeling extreme weakness. I have to stay hospitalized another day or two—no question. Bob comes in, hands me eight envelopes. There's two thousand dollars in each of them.

«What's this for,» I ask, surprised.

«For getting these guys arrested—you know, crime stoppers,» he says with a smirk.

«Can't take it—you know that,» I respond.

«Why not?»

«Think about it. Where did all the money come from? Everybody knows I'm broke.»

«Your uncle just died, right?»

«Yeah, a few months ago. Okay, I get it. I guess he could have left it to me.»

«See you soon, and for God's sake take it easy!» Bob commands while putting the money on the bed.

«Sure,» I mutter under my breath, because he is already gone. I've been offered money before, but I refused it.

The thought of my uncle's death brings to mind Louisa's death. Suddenly the grief is right in front of me; but before it takes over, anger replaces it.

God, I gotta get out of here for a bit! I grab a wheelchair and go outside for a smoke. What a mistake—it's so hard to quit. The fresh air makes me feel better. This is going to be easier than I thought. I have money in my pocket and a clearer way of thinking. Tomorrow I am getting the hell out of here!

I go into the hospital and phone Frank, ask him to pick Margaret up and come get me tomorrow morning. On the table by the phone there's a newspaper and a story about me being shot, recovering in St. Paul's hospital, getting released soon.

Chapter 9

Going out the door in the morning, Frank is pushing the wheelchair. Margaret is holding my hand. I hear the sound of a gun going off. Out of the corner of my eye I see chips fly out of a brick on the wall by the door. Shit, that was close!

«Somebody's fucking shooting at us,» Frank yells.

«Jesus Christ, what's going on?» I freak out as Frank pulls me back inside with Margaret right behind. Turning around in the wheelchair, I look across the street and see Mike running away, giving us the finger. Apparently, nobody is willing to sell to Mike anymore. He's strung out on heroin, living in a dump, angry, and broke. He must have seen the newspaper and was just waiting for me to come out.

«He blames us for the mess he is. Guess he just lost it,» Frank mutters, shaking his head.

Cops arrive. Their questions come a mile a minute. «What, who, when, why, where was the shot from?» all the important questions.

We hear another shot, this time sounding a little muffled, but nothing whizzes past my head. Three cops carefully race over to where they heard the shot fired. Mike is found slumped over behind some bushes. He's shot himself; he had put the rifle in his mouth and blown his brains out—poor Mike.

It seems like hours before we are finished being

questioned by the police, only to be told we might be needed again soon. Fuck, will this stop for a while? I'm all used up, not much left to give.

We go to Frank's. He wants us to stay with him for a while.

I'm lying in the guest room trying to sleep, thinking about Mike, listening to the radio. A Robbie Robertson song comes on, «Somewhere down The Crazy River.» The song has a line in it that fits me to a tee, «The wind just seemed to push me that way.»

In my case, all it takes is a gentle breeze—no direction, no thought to where I am going. I never think about the future. I live in the here and now, the next hit, next blowjob, the next anything—but never tomorrow. I guess I've never thought I'd be around for very long.

There's something I've never really done, come to terms with some of my past. The last time I was in the hospital was what gave me the strength to finally do what I'm trying to do now. I'd been up for five straight days doing crack and was so wired I was hearing voices and seeing things. I got it in my head that people were after me. I got in the car and started to drive to Whistler Mountain. I was «being followed» by every car behind me. I was going as fast as the car would go.

The Squamish Highway has a lot of twists and turns, cliffs, and switchbacks like every mountain road. In front of me a car slammed on its brakes at a stoplight. I was going so fast I could not stop in time. I swerved around him only to find a school bus in my way. I swerved again. My bumper hit the bumper of the bus, and my car started to spin. Thinking I was going over the cliff, I released my seat belt just before I hit a tree. My head broke the window as I went through it.

My last clear memory was of being in the ambulance on the way to the hospital.

I'm walking down a hallway, doors on either side of me. A person walking beside me says, «Come on, Chris, time for meds.»

«What?»

«Time for meds.»

My mind is very unclear. I don't know what he's talking about. «Where am I?»

«UBC Psych Ward,» he says, looking at me in a strange way.

«What?» I say, not quite believing him.

«The hospital. Come on, time for meds.»

«What are you talking about? What meds?» I am really starting to freak out now.

«Come on, follow me.»

We arrive at what looks like a reception desk. A nurse hands me a little paper cup. «Here, Chris, take these. Now, please.»

«What are they? I'm not gonna take them.»

She looks at me and sees how fucked up I am. She gets on the phone, says a few words, and tells me to hold on a minute. A doctor comes up and asks, «What's the problem?»

«I'm not going to take these. What are they, and where am I?» My head is still very foggy, so hard to concentrate. «Where am I? Why am I here?»

He takes me aside and asks, «What do you feel like? What's going on?»

«Like there are three or four people in my head, all of them talking at once.»

«You were in a car accident. The pills are to make you calm,» he explains.

«How long have I been here?» I ask as calmly as I can.

«Four days.»

I freak out. My head clears from the shock. «How long have I been taking them?» I ask, pointing at the pills.

«The whole four days, three times a day.»

«Well, I'm not taking them anymore,» I say, horror and revulsion in my voice and on my face.

«Okay, we'll see how you behave. If you act up, I'll have to insist. Lunch is ready. Eat, and we'll talk after.»

I follow somebody to the cafeteria. Everybody seems to know me. «Hey, Chris, sit here.»

I go over and sit down. «Who are you?» I ask.

«I'm your roommate,» he says. «What wrong with you?»

I do not know what to say or do. Four fucking days, and I don't remember any of it. I feel almost normal after a few coffees. However, I keep hearing voices whispering to me. They're in my head, talking in my ear. I'm the sort of person who won't let people see if I am fearful, happy, or sad. That's how I was able to make the doctors think I was starting to become normal.

The doctor comes up to me and asks me again, «Why won't you take the pills?»

«They won't let me be me. I don't remember the last four days at all,» I tell him.

«We'll watch you for the next few days, see how you are. Is that okay?»

«Sure.»

Over the next few days I find out some of the things I had been saying and doing. What a freak show. Two days later the doctor visits me and says, «You seem to be doing much better. You don't have to take the pills anymore. You've been committed to the ward, though, and cannot leave until I think you are well enough.»

I'm feeling so fucked up over this I want to hit him. I'm the one who has to be in control. How can I fix this? I tell the doctor how much I hate being told what to do and how to act.

«If you see a few bad reactions from me, that's the reason for it, not because I'm getting out of control!» The voices were always in my head. I was learning how to ignore them. I was there a month, but the only way I would be allowed to leave was if I went to a treatment center for another month. It was at the treatment center that I find out it was Bill who had run Louisa over. And it was an intentional murder.

At the treatment center they search all my baggage and then take me to my bed. It's a dormitory, one side for men, the other for women. The very first person I see is Margaret, who I had not seen for years. I had invited her to the wedding, but she did not come. She runs up to me and gives me a very warm hug and kiss. She's not looking too good, skinny and very shaky.

«Oh Chris, am I glad to see you. I was going to leave, but now you're here maybe I'll be all right.»

«Man, I'm glad to see you too. We can help each other. I guess you've heard how fucked up I've been?»

«Yeah, I was very sorry to hear about Louisa.»

«It took a lot out of me, nearly everything.»

We hear over the PA that it's lunch. She takes my hand, and we go to the lunchroom. I see Bill, and he's sitting with somebody I have seen around but do not know. He pretends not to notice me, but his face turns a little white. After lunch we go into the TV room. There are couches and side chairs. I am very excited by Margaret's presence, remembering what we had before. I tell her about my accident, and hearing voices, all of it. She holds my hand, and I just know things will be okay.

After a few days when you finish detoxing, you start feeling more energetic and start getting horny. At least we did. We looked for a place to get a little privacy. The TV room is usually empty because the TV is broken, so it is perfect. One couch is under a bookcase, leaving a space between it and the wall. At one end is another wall, at the other end a big flowerpot with a large bushy plant in it. I look behind it, and there is enough room for both of us lying side by side. We hide there every day for a week, almost getting caught a few times.

One afternoon we are there just holding each other when we hear two male voices. As they get a little closer I recognize Bill's voice and the guy I had seen him hanging around with. They sit on the couch we're hiding behind. Their voices are very quiet, but we are only inches away, so we hear clearly what they are talking about. I'm afraid they will hear our breathing. Bill is talking.

«Man, when I saw Chris come in I really started to get scared.»

«Me too. Do you think he knows what we did to his wife?»

«Quiet, man. Do you want someone to hear?»

What's going on? What did they do to Louisa? I start to get up. Margaret grabs me and puts a finger to her lips.

«Art, you gotta be careful. Nobody can find out about this,» Bill says.

«Man, we killed his wife?»

My heart misses a beat. My muscles tense as I start to get up. Margaret grabs me again.

«We were supposed to kill his brother's wife. How did we know they had a similar name? Gordon never told us who she was, or why he wanted her dead.»

What's this? They killed her by mistake? My brother's wife had a similar name, Louise. My brother and his wife were junkies. Who's Gordon?

«Too bad the ten grand went so fast.»

The shock was too much. I was frozen, unable to move. A mistake! My life was ruined because of a mistake?

«We can't even tell Gordon we got the wrong bitch.»

«Well, Gordon was just our contact. I don't know who wanted her dead.»

«I think I know who it is.»

«Don't tell me. I don't want to know,» Bill interjects.

«It's okay, Bill. You don't know them.»

«I'm going for a smoke. You coming?»

«Yeah.»

No wonder my brother left. He must know they were after Louise. They leave. I'm so stunned I can't even move.

Margaret starts whispering in my ear how sorry she is. «We'll make everything okay. We'll fix it. What do you want to do?»

«Kill them; make them pay. They got ten grand for making a mistake.»

«Mark must have known it was his Louise that was supposed to be killed. All this time, and he didn't tell me.» Mark is my brother.

«We have to get out of here, Chris. While they are out having a smoke, we gotta get out of here. Before they come back in—weak fucking pansies. If they see us in here, they'll know we heard them,» Margaret exclaims.

«Yeah, you're right,» I tell her.

Later, back on my bed in the treatment center, I'm still in shock, but my mind is turning to revenge, full of hate. Gonna find this Gordon guy, kill 'em all. I have to find Mark and see if he knows Gordon. Here I am, no money, wearing another man's clothes. How can I do this? I guess it's time to start setting people up.

I finally made up my mind. I stayed for the whole month, and by the time I left my resolve was strong and I knew what to do. Margaret said she would help; she had a bit of money. There were no voices anymore.

Bill left that same afternoon. Lucky for him or me—I'm not sure which. Have to find out a lot more about Art and his friend. He is going to die before Bill does!

Chapter 10

I wake up in Frank's spare room feeling really mixed up and confused. I need to get to an NA meeting.

As I head downstairs to call a cab, Frank says, «Where are you going? Margaret went out but will be back soon with some takeout.»

«Got to go to a meeting,» I tell him

«Well, she wanted you to wait for her.»

«No, I have to go. Feeling like getting high, and I don't need that,» I tell him.

«There's a meeting down the road. Come on. I'll give you a ride,» Frank offers.

Just then, the cab arrives. I tell Frank, «It's here. I may as well take it.» He walks me to the cab and tells the driver where the meeting is.

I need to be around people who know me. I give the cabby a different address. It's a meeting I usually do not go to, but I know a lot of people who do. Walking in the door, I notice a girl who looks familiar. She looks at me, turns to the woman beside her and says something. I see it is Margaret she is talking to and I wave at her. The girl beside her gets up. She runs over and gives me a big hug. I look at her and suddenly realize it's the girl that was being forced into prostitution. I did not think she would remember who I was. I thought she knew nothing about me.

Margaret walks up to me, a weird expression on her face. It was a mixture of guilt and maybe a little relief. I'm very confused. How do they know each other? «Well, I see the cat is out of the bag,» Margaret grins.

«What did you say?» I reply, still confused.

«I want you to meet my sister, Amy.»

«Your sister?»

«Not here, let's go for a coffee.»

I look at them closely. They do have a similar look about them, one much younger, but the resemblance is there. Margaret is looking as if she's been taken off guard and is trying to think how to explain what is going on. We get in her car in silence and go to a restaurant. After ordering coffees all around, I ask what is going on.

«I guess it's time to tell you some things. I'll explain my part and Amy's in this, but it's all good,» Margaret smiles.

I look at Amy, who smiles at me and nods. Margaret starts talking again and asks me not to interrupt. She takes a sip of coffee trying to decide where to start. «Well, I guess the story starts when mom and dad died. I tried my best to be there for Amy, but I was only fifteen myself. Amy was ten. Social services put her in foster care until I turned eighteen. Amy withdrew, became quiet, and kept to herself. She went to school and did pretty well just drifting along, no close friends. When she got to high school she seemed to come out of her shell, interested in boys, and wanting to be with other people. I was so happy about the new Amy that I did not notice all the changes. She was coming out of her shell. One day I was putting away her laundry, and I found a fold of cocaine. I confronted her, and I guess you can imagine what went on.

«I grounded her and was on the phone asking Frank

what I should do. He said he was coming right over, and to hang on a bit. I went up to her room. The window was open, and she was not there. I did not see her for eight months. Frank and I went searching, could not find her. We went to the police, and they started looking for her also. One day we got a knock on the door, and your friend Bob was there. Bob seemed to know Frank.

«Bob said, 'I have something to show you. Where's your computer? This is going to hurt. It's very personal. It concerns Amy.'

«He slipped a memory stick in the computer, clicked a few times. On the screen a guy was doing something with a white powder, mixing another powder in with it. He went into the next room where Amy was sitting on the couch. She was only fifteen. He walked up to her and said, 'Here, it's the best coke there is. Watch out. It will knock you on your ass!' She opened the fold and did a few hits.

«At that point Amy said, 'God this is good,' and then slowly fell over unconscious.» Margaret is shaking her head.

«The bastard got up, went over to her, took her clothes off, admired her a bit and then proceeded to rape her. After he was finished, he carefully dressed her and woke her up. He told her to 'Get lost.'

«Then Bob got up, fast forwarded to another scene very similar to the first. All in all the asshole raped her eight times. Finally, we saw footage of Amy talking with this guy, and she was begging him for some more coke. He told her, 'You owe me a thousand dollars. You want more? I want a blowjob, and I want it now.'

«She got on her knees and did it. When he was finished, he gave her a fold, and she did some. After a few minutes she said, 'This is different. I want the stuff you gave me before.'

He told her to 'do some more.' She did and said, 'It's not the same.'

«She started feeling shaky and begged for the other blow. The man came over to her and told her, 'You know that was coke mixed with heroin, at first just a little but now almost all heroin. You want more—you do what I say. You belong to me now.' He called out, 'Come in here.' Another man walked in, went over to Amy, pulled his penis out, told Amy to suck it. Amy said no. The first man went over, hit Amy, and said, 'Suck it.'

«Amy said, 'Fuck you.'

«The bastard backhanded her across the face. She tried to run and almost made it to the door. He caught her and slapped her around a lot, but careful not to mark her up too badly. Amy finally gave in. Then they both raped her. Beaten and broken, Amy lay in a slump on the floor. The man handed her a flap with almost pure heroin inside. She did some. The man told her, 'Here are the ground rules. You do what I say, when I say, and do it with anyone I say, no back talk.' He told her to 'Come back tomorrow, or I will find you and kill you. You're mine now.'

«Amy got up and left. The two men talked a bit, and then both went out. Another face appeared so close he got blurry, and then the screen went blank.»

Margaret says, «It was your face, Chris.» She clears her throat and then continues. «Bob stuck another memory stick in the computer. Your picture appeared again, your hand upraised as though putting something away. You looked very angry.

«'Who the fuck are you?' a voice said.

«'Somebody you don't want to know,' you said, then you walked up to him, kicked him in the balls, and when he doubled over, you kneed him in the face. You continued to hit almost every part of his body. 'You sold me coke mixed with heroin, and I planted a camera here to see what was going on. I saw what you did to that girl, and I should kill you,' you told him. 'But you are going to prison where I know some people, and you are going to be theirs.'

«A few minutes later Bob showed up with Amy behind him. You wandered around the apartment looking it over, and there were whips, chains, cuffs, and a lot of other things hanging from the wall like blindfolds and ball gags. It was a BDSM room.

«Bob arrested the man. 'What a prick,' you said about the guy.

«Bob looked right into the camera and took out the memory card. You tried to stop him, but he wouldn't give it back,» Margaret says.

«The look on your face when you looked at Amy, such hurt and concern. Even a look that said you wanted to help. Now you know why Frank came by to see you that day. Why I came by to bring that coke to you. I had to meet this man so full of kindness and compassion. You saved my sister from something too horrible to imagine. I came by to thank you, but you were such a nice man I wanted to get to know you and help you. Frank has been watching out for you since before that day.

«Now that you know this part, it's up to Frank to tell you his,» Margaret finishes her story.

All this time Amy is looking at me with tears in her eyes, and says, «I am so glad you know. Now it's my turn to be able to thank you and be able to get to know you.»

We grow silent, taking it all in. We finish our coffee and leave. We all go to Frank's for dinner. They want to talk about it more, but I postpone for a while, needing some time to get my head around it. Margaret says she is going to take a bath, so I turn to Frank and say, «I'll talk with you tomorrow. This has taken a new turn, and I need to digest it a bit.»

«Okay,» Frank says.

Amy gets up, gives me a hug, and says, «Thanks. I'll see you tomorrow.»

Chapter 11

I'm watching her in the bath. Margaret does not know I am there. She thinks I am still downstairs with Frank. I watch her wash herself, and then she feels between her legs.

«Oh shit,» she mutters. She gets her razor off the shelf and starts to shave her pussy because she knows that is what I like. She finishes, and I can see her hand lingering, her fingers slowly rubbing her clit. I'm getting really aroused watching her. She continues to masturbate, and I think I have to stop her before she reaches climax. I walk away from the door a few feet and make a small sound, enough to get her attention but not enough to alarm her. It works; she stops masturbating, gets out of the bath, and dries off.

Margaret knows I like lingerie, so she picks up her new see-through, pale blue harem costume. The panties are crotch less, the opening wide so her mound shows very clearly. She knows if she wears this to bed I will want her as badly as she wants me. «If I go to sleep, it will feel like a shorter time until he comes upstairs,» she says in a low whisper to herself.

I wait until I hear her breathing slowly, and her slight movements stop. She is asleep, lying on top of the covers with her legs slightly apart. The sight of her lying there, her perfect breasts slightly hidden by the sheer blue fabric, her crotch so beautiful, hairless, slightly moist and looking so inviting. I walk softly to the bed and slowly start to lick and kiss her legs, lingering on her thighs, slowly circling her now juicy clit and vagina.

Her hands by now are on my head, pulling me closer, trying to position my mouth on her hard pulsing clit. I start to lick and softly suck it. She starts to shudder, and I know her climax is near. I stop and slowly kiss and lick her stomach, working my way up to her nipples. I lick and suck on each one until they are very big and hard, squeezing one nipple gently and sucking on the other, licking the tip. I reach for her hand and put it on her clit.

«Play,» I encourage. She starts to masturbate. I leave my finger on top of hers so I can be sure of how she wants to be played with this time. We have known each other a long, very intimate time. I slowly start to kiss my way to her clit watching her play with herself. I bring my cock around to her mouth. She sees it and gasps as she realizes how hard it is and how in need of release I am.

I see her thigh muscles beginning to quiver and know her time is near. I remove her hand and put my cock in her mouth. She kisses and licks the head, now sucking and licking the head, the escaping liquid making her arousal even more intense. She is shivering, and I know it is not from the cold. I slowly lick and suck on her clit, stopping and starting, always bringing her to the brink of orgasm, never letting her quite achieve it.

«If you want to cum, you will have to let me cum in your mouth, swallow, and then beg me, 'your master,' to let you cum,» I command her. She is very willing to do just this. She sucks harder and harder. Suddenly I explode in her mouth. She swallows and screams.

«Oh master. You are my master. Please, master!» She

shudders uncontrollably with one of the best orgasms of her life, collapses into my arms. «You are my master. I am totally in your control,» she whispers, reaching down again for my cock. Her soft hands harden my cock yet again. It is going to be a long, lust-filled night.

Margaret had always been submissive to me, doing whatever I asked. It was a very big turn-on in many respects, but there was always a measure of guilt for me. I think there are some things in her past that I do not know about. She seems to be happy and enjoys my company very much. She has even told me she loves me. She can be secretive about things. I have always thought it was because of her drug addiction and the things it had made her do.

All I know is that her love, no, just her presence, has returned me to sanity, giving me the hope and resolve to continue on my chosen path. If she wants to have a few secrets, that is okay with me. I know that will change with time.

Chapter 12

In the morning I go downstairs for a coffee. Frank is there waiting for me. There is a spring in my step as I remember the night before and a smile on my face.

«Good to see you smile,» Frank says, which brings a bigger smile to my face. «I guess we need to talk.»

«Yeah, I guess we do. Let me get a coffee first.» Reluctantly letting the memory of the night before go I bring my mind back to the present.

Sitting down across the table from Frank, he gives me a smile. «Well,» he says. «I'm glad it's finally come out, and we can be honest with you and show our gratitude in a real way and not behind your back.» He is looking at me as if thinking, How to start?

«There's more to this than you might imagine, besides your saving our Amy. Another person is involved that might surprise you. Don't worry. It is all good. We have your best interests at heart. There is somebody coming over, and there is much to talk about. He will be here shortly, and we will explain it all. In the meantime, I have to tell you that I can never repay you for what you did for Amy and for all the rest, how sad and angry I am over the death of Louisa. That is part of what we want to talk to you about.»

«I thought Amy was in and out of foster homes a lot of her life?» I ask him.

«Until Margaret was old enough to look after her, but she had been in four or five foster homes for three or four years. It did her a lot of harm,» Frank explains.

«How is she adjusting to life now?» I ask.

«She is doing quite well, goes to meetings, and is seeing a shrink. I really do not know what good that is; they seem to be as sick as their patients are. She has always wanted to be able to thank you herself. She had to be satisfied that we were looking out for you.

«There are going to be a few surprises coming your way in the next little while. I want you to know that other people were behind a lot of the decisions that were made. Your well-being and support are very important to all of us.»

I'm getting really curious wondering what's going on. The doorbell rings. Frank answers the door, and as he steps aside, I see Bob coming in.

He shakes Frank's hand, says, «I'm glad this moment is finally here. We can pool our thoughts and information more freely now.» He gives me a big grin. «Guess this is a big surprise for you, eh?» Bob says.

«Hell, much more than that, but I'm not all that surprised. Frank seemed to know more about me than he should have. This explains a lot.»

Frank grins and says, «Me and Bob go way back. We went to the police academy together. He's my boss.» I sit back in my chair, trying to take it all in. I thought I knew Frank. He did coke, drank, and partied with the best or the worst of us.

He gives me a look, seeming to know what I was thinking and says, «Think back. The coke you saw me snort always came out of a fold from my pocket. Think about it.» He winks so Bob cannot see. He did do a bit of coke with me, when it was mine. Guess he did not want Bob to know about that.

«Even when I gave him a mirror with a line or two on it for him he would say, 'Nah, it's too strong. I like it a little weaker. I'll do my own,'» I tell Bob, effectively keeping Frank's secret.

«He also drank like a fish but never seemed to be really drunk. Taking the story a little farther.»

«Mostly 7-up or Sprite,» he said. «A little booze just so you could smell it if you wanted.» This was another little lie. I mixed drinks for him, and he drank them all. I guess everyone has a secret or two. In Frank's case it was because he wanted to keep his job. Who was I to be his judge?

I look at Bob and ask, «Why wasn't I put in jail? I sold Frank two ounces when we first met.»

«I had been talking to Frank about you for years, and I told him what a good guy you were, that you were basically an honest guy, willing to help anybody. You had a problem with cocaine, but you also had a very moral side, and that you were my friend,» Bob explained.

«So Frank knew about me even before I helped Amy?» I ask looking at them both.

«Yeah, I asked him to look after you a bit. I was really worried about you. I told him about your little sideline a little before Bill shot you. That was just between you and me, Chris. It was getting too complicated keeping Frank out of the picture. It was also safer for you,» Bob explains.

«Frank brought that coke to me. I did not want to arrest you, so we decided to give it back. It turns out to have been a very good decision. That is why Margaret turned up with it at your door. I guess she really started to like you.»

What else do they have to tell me? This is already

enough. I was trying to think of the implications. Where did I fit in with all they were telling me?

Seeing the look on my face, Bob and Frank both start to talk at the same time and then grin at each other. Frank points at Bob as if to say, «you start.»

«Frank has been undercover for four or five years. You made it very easy for him to infiltrate certain drug rings, knowing who was involved and how, their habits, and who was in a position for us to use. Money or a pass on being prosecuted was their incentive,» Bob clarifies.

Frank had also been planting wireless video cameras in various places, often finding out that you had beat him to it. When Bill was killed, it took us by surprise. Up until then the pattern had been to beat them up, then cut all ties with them. Believe me, Frank would not have left if he had thought they would kill him.»

Thank God you did leave. I wanted him dead, and dead he is.

Bob continued, «We now believe he was killed because of his involvement in Louisa's death. They knew how much blow he had been doing, how mentally deranged the drugs had made him become. They figured he was too big a liability.»

«Makes sense,» I say. «He was in a very bad way.»

«Another thing that's going to surprise you,» Bob says. «Mike was also murdered, and he was not the one who took a shot at you. We thought it might be the other person who was in detox with Bill. Art, wasn't it?»

«I think so. I was really fucked up about what I'd heard. Margaret will know for sure,» I shrug.

«There was powder residue on Mike, and the partial fingerprint on the rifle was not his,» Frank interjects. «There are a lot of people looking for him. You will not be safe until he is found. No more meetings for you for a while, okay?»

«Sure,» I agree. «With all this going on getting high is the last thing on my mind. I feel stoned already what with all that is going on.»

Thinking about Mike, I realize that he'd been doing heroin as well as cocaine. I mention it to Bob and Frank. «I've been concentrating my efforts on coke dealers. Maybe I needed to change my focus. We should look at the footage of Mike and Bill see if there is a connection. Maybe we should change the direction of our efforts. The heroin mixed with the coke makes me think there are different dealers involved,» I suggest thoughtfully.

«We have just finished cataloguing the videos and can pull the ones of Mike and Bill.» Bob brings out his cell phone, talks a few minutes, hangs up, and says, «It will take a while, but they will be waiting in my office when I get back there.

«We have been noticing a lot of overdoses where the cause of death is a mixture of coke and heroin. We have been discussing this and have alerted our undercover officers to be aware of and look for these new sources. I have to go now; you and Frank have a lot to discuss anyway. I'll let you get to it. I'll get back to you tonight or tomorrow sometime. Now we are together on this, it might go a lot quicker. See you later.»

When Bob leaves, Frank and I sit at the kitchen table drinking coffee and talking.

«You know Mike was a friend of my brother. Maybe he is the common link in all this. He knew Bill also. Maybe looking at the videos is the answer,» I suggest.

Frank looks thoughtful and says, «That makes sense. I have met some of Mike and Bill's friends myself, and they never quite belonged with most of the other dealers. They knew one another but never really hung out. I think we are on to something here.»

I hand Frank a couple of videos and say, «Check these out.»

Just then, Margaret and Amy come into the room. They both walk over to me. Margaret gives me a hug and a kiss. With the offer of breakfast, they wander to the stove. I go for a shower, a new bounce in my step. I'm feeling surprisingly good, the pain and depression lifted. I have a new hope that I will reach some solution to this mess.

After breakfast, I decide to get some exercise. These past weeks and months have taken their toll on me. I have always been strong, having had a lot of manual labour jobs. I have lost a lot of weight but am now quickly gaining it back. If I want to gain muscle instead of fat, I have to work out. I ask Frank if he has any physical work needing to be done, the harder the better. He gets me pruning his hedge. It goes all the way around his property. He offers me a gas-powered trimmer, but I decide to use hand clippers, wanting to build up my arms. The hedge is so big it takes four days, the raking two more. By the time I am finished, I hurt like hell but already can see and feel the difference in my arms, chest, and back. At night I use his rowing machine and treadmill. After the hedge is done, I chop down a few trees and split logs for the fireplace.

I keep that routine up for the next four weeks and now feel better than I have in years. The craving for coke is nonexistent. I don't miss it at all. The three of us, Frank, Bob, and I get together and view the videos. There are about five people that we had met before. One of them is the son of my old boss, who knew of my problem with drugs, and told me that if I cleaned up I could have my old job back. The three of us decide that is a good place for us to start our new plan. We also decide to leave Amy and Margaret out of it.

I read a lot of detective stories, and in a lot of them the hero neglects to protect his family. I am not going to let that happen. I make it clear that they are to be protected at all costs, or I will not be involved. Otherwise, I will simply disappear and do things my own way, not be involved with the police at all. The novels always have the hero rescuing his loved ones from the bad guy, not me. The reason I had not done anything before was worrying about my family.

When I was in active addiction, I did not socialize with anybody. My dope was delivered whenever possible so I was out of practice in talking with people. Surprisingly, I feel no unease at being with these three people. They make me feel at home, knowing what is needed before I do. Making love at night is one of the most normal and wonderful things I've done in years. I'm turning into the person I had never been but had always wanted to be. It's a wonderful time, normalizing, healing, and cleansing. There's a new purpose, a new clarity in my mind. There's also a very controlled anger. I cannot get over this feeling—normalcy. What a strange and wonderful way to live.

The most important thing I feel so far is the very strong feeling that I can actually trust these people. To a drug addict trust is something that does not exist. The only thing you trust is your drug. You know exactly what it is going to do to you. Even knowing it is all bad does not stop your using.

About a month after our first meeting, the three of us think it is time to start in our new direction. Bob tells me there is an apartment he knows about, a short distance from my old shop. He will arrange for the use of it. Hopefully I will be able to get my old job back. During the previous month Bob's undercover men gained a good idea of who the minor players were, and maybe a couple who were a little higher up. It seems my old boss's son is heavily involved.

That morning I go to see my old boss. The reception I get is very surprising. When he sees me he gets up, shakes my hand, puts his arm on my shoulder and squeezes. It is a more intimate gesture than I like from a man, and a chill runs down my back. What's this? Is the guy gay? I look at him and do not get the sense that it's a sexual gesture but one of real, pleased surprise. As we talk, I get the sense there is some underlying emotion behind his words. Is it my imagination, or is it guilt?

He asks how I am doing, and I tell him I'm doing really well. «Clean and sober, living by myself, with no attachments, an apartment a few blocks away.» That is the story we had decided on. To my surprise he offers me a job without my having to ask. Even though I knew I was good at my job, the five-dollar-an-hour raise was a surprise. He offers an advance on my pay, saying he thought I might be broke.

«I heard about your wife, and that you had been trying to end it all with drugs. Glad to see you changed your mind. You are too good a person to leave us so soon. When do you want to start?»

«How about today, maybe after lunch, work up to a full day by the end of the week? It's been a long while since I had a real job.»

«Sounds good to me,» he says. «See you at 12:30?»

«Great,» I reply, heading out the door.

I want to start work as soon as possible, but I needed to arrange the apartment with Bob. I plan to invite Randy, who is the boss' son, over that very day. The people mixing the heroin into the coke are going to suffer.

Feeling good about the progress so far today, I go to

Bob's to arrange for the apartment. He is in the kitchen cleaning his gun. I look at him and the gun; he looks at me and says, «I clean it when I'm in here and not eating. If people are over, it's my way of telling them 'I'm in charge.' I have a very clean gun.»

«I bet,» I grin. «I got the job, so now I need the apartment. I want to bring Randy by tonight, start everything in motion. Will it be possible to get it today, the apartment I mean?»

«Oh yeah, I arranged it this morning. There are some people over there right now fixing it up,» he tells me.

«Great, it's all going pretty good, don't you think?» I ask him.

«Yes,» he says with some satisfaction. «It's going really well, better than I had hoped. I mean you are doing better than I had hoped. I'm really proud of you, Chris,» he tells with a lot of warmth in his voice. «I was really worried about you for a very long time.»

I do not know how to react. I'm not used to this kind of talk. It's time to go. «Thanks, no need to worry any more I think. I have it under control now,» I say—and I actually believe it myself.

«I think so too, Chris. Keep it up. What you are doing is very important, but please be careful. You're not a cop, and nobody expects you to be the hero,» he pleads.

«No worries, I'm just a druggie trying to do something good for a change. I'm no hero,» I say with all sincerity. «I have to go now, to work. Do you know how strange that feels coming from my lips? I haven't said that for a very long time.»

He walks me to the door and gives me a pat on the shoulder.

I'm on my way.

Chapter 13

The apartment is mine. It is only one-and-a-half blocks from my new job. The key is under the mat by the front door. The manager is a friend of Frank's. If anybody asks questions, he knows what to say. Margaret has been asked to stay away for now and is not supposed to know what the address is. I know it will be hard to stay away from her, but to see her in danger is not going to happen either.

I go to work, and it's as if I never left. All the same people work here, except one new guy in charge of shipping and receiving.

I start getting friendly with Randy. We had gotten high and drunk together many times in the past, gone to pubs, played pool, and even had a few of the same girls. It was easier to get friendly with him again than I thought it would be. He even suggested he come by my place, «Maybe go play some pool or something.»

Randy seemed to be a little high all the time. Most people would not notice, but for me it was easy to spot. I've been around people who do coke and heroin and know the signs. Heroin makes you look drowsy; you nod off and go to never-never land. With coke mixed in it keeps you awake and aware.

After work, I give Randy my address. I tell him to come by in an hour or so and go to check out my new apartment.

As I open the door, I see a couple of my jackets hanging on a hook. Going to the bedroom, I see an unmade bed, some of my clothes strewn on the floor, in the dresser more of my clothes. Moving to the kitchen there are some dirty dishes, a few plates, cutlery, five or six coffee cups, and half a pot of cold coffee.

I open the fridge—half a carton of milk, a few veggies. The freezer holds hamburger, a few steaks, and pork chops. On the kitchen table there's another half-empty coffee cup. The living room has a nice sized TV, a comfortable couch, and a few chairs. They all look as if I might have picked them myself. On the coffee table is an envelope. Inside are twenty one hundred dollar bills and thirty twenty dollar ones. A note reads, «Enjoy.» Man, they got this place looking perfect. The apartment is exactly like ones I've lived in many times before, but not quite as messy. Time will take care of that!

I turn on the TV and notice there is even a bit of dust on it. The channel is the one I watch most of the time. Looking for the remote, I cannot find it. Perfect! I lie down on the couch, kick my shoes and socks off. They land on the floor next to a pair already there. This is getting freaky. I feel something under the pillow, the remote, exactly where it ends up when I use it. Whoever set this place up certainly knows me.

Lying on the couch, I think of the day at work and the people there. They seemed quieter, somehow, more subdued than before. They were like Randy in a way, but more so. Were they high? I will find out soon. A dangerous place for me if they are.

My intercom rings. It's Randy. I buzz him in, and he arrives carrying a six-pack of Pepsi. «I remember you drink this,» he says, handing it to me. «I would have brought beer, but Dad says you are staying clean and sober. Want to play pool somewhere, or rent a movie? I see you have a DVD player.»

«Let's go play pool,» I reply. «We can go to the pub, and its okay for you to have a beer. If it gets too much for me, I'll go home. I'm a bit tired anyway, not used to working yet.»

We go out the door. He heads over to a brand new Jeep. I walk around and admire it. «Wow, nice. How much this set you back?»

«A thousand down, six hundred bucks a month,» he says.

«I guess you make enough to afford it?»

«Yeah, Dad gave me a raise, but a lot more work goes with it. I can't complain,» he tells me, bragging. He seems more his normal self, not stoned.

Once we are at the bar, I get some change for the pool table while Randy goes to the washroom. I rack the balls. When he comes out of the bathroom, I can tell he's high. This is going to be harder than I thought.

He breaks, misses, and I step up to the table. I'm pissed off that he got high, and I run the table. We play for an hour. He disappears to the washroom every twenty minutes or so. Finally, I tell him I have to leave, but he's nodding off at our table. He's been doing coke and heroin, and the heroin is finally taking over.

This time I shake his shoulder hard and tell him, «I gotta go.»

«Okay, see you tomorrow,» he mumbles. I'm angry he got high when he knew I was trying to stay clean. What a fucking waste of time and effort.

When I arrive home, Frank is waiting for me at the door. As we go upstairs he says, «You know the guy who raped Amy? I've got some news on him.»

«Good.» We go inside my apartment. He sits in the easy chair, me on the couch. «Don't leave me hanging!»

«I talked with an inmate of his. He said the guy's teeth have been knocked out, one tooth at a time, with a hammer and nail punch. Done carefully, so his jawbone would remain nice and smooth. The other inmates love it. They say it feels good,» he reports, almost laughing. «I'm told they took five days to take them out, about twenty minutes a tooth. He was conscious the whole time, no freezing. Must have hurt like hell.

«They say his gums healed nice and smooth, no bumps or anything. He hears the words 'suck it' so often now he thinks it's his name. He tried to kill himself, so at night he is tied up, his ass in the air. He's moved from cell to cell. He is never alone, so popular is the service he provides. He does not sit down very much. The guards do not like him much either. It's sort of a good ending to a sad story.»

«That's what I had in mind for him myself. Hopefully he will be blamed for other things to get his sentence extended.»

«That's the plan,» Frank nods.

«I think they should get him some hormones, get some boobs on him, and grow his hair. From what I remember, he was kind of ugly, but a little makeup might help. It's a fitting end for that son of a bitch,» I say, still grinning.

«Yes it is,» Frank says.

«Does Amy know any of this? She should know that he is suffering for what he did to her,» I ask.

«She knows he is getting much more than he gave, but who knows how many girls he did it to? More than one I fear.»

«Well, I hope he leads a long and not happy life,» I say with some amusement.

«I have a feeling he will be well, though not gently, taken care of,» Frank gloats.

«Can you also get your friend to question him about his sexual activities—what he is involved in? There were a lot of BDSM toys in his apartment. All look well used. There is more to him than meets the eye. I would also like to see his computers. He had two of them,» I ask Frank.

«I'll do my best on that,» he assures me.

I tell Frank about my night with Randy, about his use of blow and heroin. I let him know it was hard to be around, not because of the cravings but watching the guy nodding off, wasting his life. «He used to be fun to be around. Now he's lost in his own body and mind,» I say with disgust. But who am I to talk?

«I have a surprise for you,» Frank states with a big smile on his face. He walks over to a door I thought was a closet. He opens the door, and Margaret is standing behind it.»

«Took you long enough,» she says to Frank, running over and throwing her arms around me.

«What's this?»

«Margaret insisted she be able to see you, said she would not be without you,» Frank chuckles. «The time she spent away from you was horrible. She could not eat or sleep. When you saw her in detox, she was not looking like that because of drugs, but because of her feelings for you. She arrived at detox about four hours before you did. We knew you were being released from UBC Psych Hospital. It was her idea to be there. I think you are a very lucky man, Chris. For someone to feel that way about them is very special,» Frank finishes.

I sit there not knowing what to say. I just look at her, into her eyes, and she knows that I feel the same way. I give her a long kiss, not a sexy kiss but a loving one.

When I can find my voice I say, «Well, she can use the door but only when she knows I'm alone, and I'm told in advance. I'm very serious about her not being placed in danger. I want someone to bring her here. It is a busy building, people coming and going at all hours. Won't be too hard to fit in with them,» I say as forcefully as I can.

Margaret can see the doubt on my face, but also the desire, and being a woman she knows how to play me. She puts her hand on my thigh, slowly makes little circles with her finger. It sends electricity up and down my body, and I know I cannot say no.

I look at Frank. He knows it's time to go. At the door I tell him, «There's a new guy at work. He's not overly friendly. Going to look him over very carefully. They have a new section where they store lacquer and thinners from somewhere down in the States. When I go to get some lacquer, I have to go to this guy and ask for it. He says it's because people have been stealing it.

«I used to work at night sometimes. I had a key then. I am going to say I need to go to meetings at noon. Maybe I can make up the time after hours. I can plant some cameras then. Maybe wait a few days.»

«Okay,» Frank says. «Let me know what you find, and stick some cameras around the place, but be careful.»

I go back into the bedroom. Margaret is in bed. She waves me over. I lift the covers before undressing. She is lying there with nothing on. I start to take my shirt off.

She slides over to me. «You're taking much too long.» She undoes my belt and button, slides the zipper down, takes me in her hand, and slowly rubs up and down. She pulls me down on the bed. Lying next to her is Heaven.

Our hands start wandering over each other's bodies, never quite touching those oh so important private parts. As we kiss each other, our lips and tongues are constantly moving, in and out, our hands finally reaching those highly sensitive parts. She takes my penis in her hands and gently, slowly caresses me. I move her legs slightly apart and tease her clitoris a bit while kissing and sucking her nipples. We play like this for a long time, almost to orgasm.

I roll on top of her, slide inside of her, gently pushing myself deeper and deeper, moving my hips in a slow, circular motion, rubbing her clit. I bring her to orgasm, almost having one myself, but I stop, pumping faster and faster, a little bit harder with each thrust until her moans in my ear make it so I cannot hold my orgasm back again. I shudder and explode inside her. I fall asleep.

Margaret is a very good-looking woman, 5 feet, 4 inches tall. Before she went to detox, she had lost a lot of weight. She has done what I have, worked out as she was gaining it back. As a result her body is slim and very muscular, her pert breasts firm and jutting upwards. I cannot get enough of her.

She is not a great cook, but getting better. We like to be together, do things together, preferably at close quarters. Cooking is one thing we enjoy doing together. She will wash and cut the veggies, and I stand behind her nibbling her ear, my hands all over her body. I like playing with her breasts, tickling her thighs and finally rubbing between her legs. Quite often our dinner is put on hold until we can concentrate on food again.

In the morning she is gone, just a trace of perfume left. After coffee, I walk to work. Coming in the door, Randy's dad is waiting for me. He takes me into the office.

«Morning,» I say. «I was hoping to talk with you, also.»

«You first,» he says.

«Well, you know I've been going to meetings, and there's a 'nooner' just down the street. I'd like to go. I'll be gone about two hours. I could make up some of the time at night. I have some bills I need to pay and could use the money.»

He looks at me a second. «Well, I was going to ask about that myself. Are you feeling good? You look good, tan, and fit.»

«Yeah, I'm good—not great, but getting there,» I say.

«Good,» he says. «There are a few things that are a bit different here. We have been importing lacquers, thinners, and other finishing supplies from the States. I have a partner in this part of the business, and they do not want people going in and out of that section of the shop. Sometimes there are a lot of drums. They are not here for long—in and out. The person working that section is their son, and to put it bluntly, he's a jerk. He has a mean streak; don't get on his bad side. If you need supplies, you have to sign for them. Okay?» he asks.

«Sounds all right with me,» I grin. «I met him yesterday, and I already don't like him.»

«Okay. Here is a key to the shop. It won't open the storage section, so make sure you get the supplies you might need before it's locked up.»

«Okay, is that all?

«Yes. Also, I just want you to know how sorry I am about your troubles; and if you need anything, you come to me! All right?» he says, sincerity in his voice.

«Sure, but I think I'll be good,» I respond, patting his shoulder.

I leave and go into the woodworking shop. There's a really smashed-up cabinet there, pieces missing, the carvings all messed up—just the kind of job I like. I need some spray lacquer and powdered colours, glue, and wood filler.

I go over to the supply room and tell him what I need. He gives me a look I do not like and wanders away. I look around wanting to find a place I can drill a hole from the other side for cameras. I realize I will need at least two locations in order to see the entire area, maybe even three. The place is spotless. I will have to be careful to leave no trace.

I figure it will take at least two or maybe three nights to get the cameras in place. My frustration with all this is the time it takes to set things up. I like things to be immediate. After all, I am a druggie, and when I want something, I want it now! I am finding I get very excited about this kind of thing. The risk of being caught is intoxicating. Sometimes I even want to get caught so I can beat the shit out of someone. I like to think I'm not a violent person by nature, but these scumbags deserve it.

I spend the rest of the day working and thinking. It's mostly about Margaret at first, then gradually about why I am here. The common thing is drugs—not just coke, as I had thought. Heroin was also in the picture. I am not too familiar with heroin dealers, but I know they overlap, especially now, since they are mixing the two.

My brother's wife was a junkie and a prostitute. I did not know much about her life. We lived in the same city, but her world was miles apart from mine. Her world revolved around tricks in alleys and secluded areas where she could ply her trade. My world, due to the paranoia involved with coke, was a more secluded place. Coming out when there was nobody around, in the dark, away from prying eyes. I have to find out how and where they connect. I feel they do, and the connection is not far away from me.

I leave for the noon meeting. I cannot concentrate on what is being said. My thoughts fill with questions, and there are no answers.

I return to work and finish the shift, working intensely on the smashed-up cabinet.

The boss comes over and says, «Do you know how long

that's been here? Six months, and nobody wanted to touch it. Now, thanks to you, no one would know it had been all smashed-up. God, I'm glad you're back. Keep it up,» he says excitedly.

«I like doing it. It's sort of like recycling, like I'm trying to do to myself. I'll finish it tonight, just a bit more to be done. A little more color here and there, and perhaps some more finish,» I tell the boss.

«Sounds good,» he says. «I'm leaving now. See you tomorrow. Don't work too long.»

«No, just for an hour or two. Goodnight,» I say as he walks away.

He's quite drunk, and he's not looking very happy. I leave the shop to get something to eat; when I come back, the new guy is just heading out. I haven't even asked his name because I do not want to get to know him. I wait in the dark. I don't want him to know I'm there. As soon as I slip inside, I get the few materials to finish the cabinet. Basically, the job is done, just a bit of lacquer here and there, perhaps two minutes work altogether.

Once I am done with the cabinet, I focus my attention on hiding the cameras. I find the drill and a vacuum to suck up the sawdust. It takes a few minutes to install, and a few more to adjust the lens to the proper angle. I am done in less than ten minutes. I decide to place another camera. As I drill the new hole, I hear a key in the lock. I jump down, run over to the workbench, and lay the drill down.

A voice behind me immediately says, «What the fuck are you doing here?»

Acting surprised, I reply, «Just finishing this cabinet. What's it to you?»

«You're not supposed to be here. A lot of valuable stuff

is here, and I don't trust you.»

«Who fucking cares what you think?» I tell him. «The boss trusts me. That's all you need to know.»

He pushes me back a few steps. I quickly grab his arm, give it a quick twist, and send him to his knees. I bring my knee up swiftly, clearly showing him I could easily bring it up to his chin. «Touch me again, fuck head, and you'll be on the floor. I do not like you, so keep your distance. Next time I talk with you it's because I want supplies. Got it?»

Something in my voice frightens him. His face goes white. He gives me one of those, «If I could you'd be dead» looks, something he cannot quite pull off, and says reluctantly, «Yeah, got it. I'll remember this.»

«Just as long as you also remember the part where you will end up on the floor,» I mock him.

«Gotta go now. Have a good night,» I say, wandering out the door.

That felt fucking wonderful! Feeling the adrenalin rush was almost like getting high. I'll have to watch out for that— don't want it to become my new drug!

Maybe not the smartest thing I've ever done, but it felt so good just the same. Perhaps it might help move things along. Before, I was working on pure anger. Now it's different. The anger is still around but very controlled. I check my coat pocket to see if the other camera is there. It is—home to bed. Despite my exhaustion, I'm still so excited from the rush. I cannot sleep so I lie on the sofa and watch TV. Three hours later I wake up, stiff as a board, and go to bed.

In the morning, I'm tired, haggard, without energy. The adrenalin I used last night has taken its toll. One thing recovering addicts need is to rest and regain their health. I need an NA meeting.

I phone work, say I will be late, and go to a morning meeting. When I get there, a guy who's obviously stoned sits beside me. That seems to happen to me all the time. I actually stopped going to meetings for a while because of it. Instead of thinking, this guy is sitting next to me to get me to use, I thought, for the very first time, Maybe he's sitting here because he knows I can help. That concept blows me away. Maybe I am getting better!

I take him for a coffee after the meeting. He tells me some of his troubles. I lend an understanding ear, give him a few suggestions, and a few phone numbers. Since my time is not my own at the moment, that's about all I can do.

Back at work, I go to get some supplies. It's a different guy there. I've seen him before somewhere. I look him over carefully, sensing I know him and not in a good way. Most of the time I am good with faces but not names.

I go over to him and say, «Hi. I'm new here and need some things. I'm Chris, by the way.»

«Oh. You're the reason I'm here today. My boss told me to take his son's place because of your little altercation last night.»

«That's great. I did not like him much. What's your name?»

«Lenny, but call me Len. I don't much like him, either.»

Hearing his voice, I know I recognize it too. It will take a while, but I'll place him. I want to be friendly with him a bit. I sense he is not a nice man, but then again I can be an asshole myself.

I say to him, «See you around, and thanks.»

«Yeah, no problem,» he says.

I go back to work wondering who he is. Getting lost in the job I am doing, I lose thoughts about him. At noon I go to another meeting. The guy I took for coffee in the morning is also there. He looks tired and wasted, but not stoned.

«Thanks for the coffee this morning, and the talk. It helped me. I phoned one of the numbers you gave me, and we're going to hook up after he gets off work.»

«Not a problem. If you need anything, here's a number you can get me at.» I give him my work business card. «I'm there until four and sometimes after six.»

He looks at the card and says, «Oh I know this place. I know a couple of guys there, Randy and Gord, the guys in charge of all the supplies. Randy is okay, but the other guy is a mean asshole.»

I'm interested in what he might tell me, but since we just met do not want to push it. «Well, call me up. We can go for a coffee again,» I tell him, meaning it.

«Yes, I will,» he says.

I can hardly wait.

Chapter 14

After work Len starts walking up the street; he walks about eight blocks to an apartment building I am familiar with. This is the building where Amy was raped. Why is Len coming in here?

I cross the street to the park. I can see into the hallway and watch Len go to the apartment where Amy was attacked. I suddenly recall the video he was in. Len was the second guy Bruce made Amy give a blowjob to. I almost lose it right then, but I know it is too soon.

What is the connection? I know I'm getting close, but close to what? Bob has taken my cameras from the apartment. I have to get back in and plant some more. I only had the one camera in the room where Amy was raped. I realize I am going to have to put one in every room. It might have to be two in the room with all the whips and things. I decide the best time will be tomorrow at lunch when I'm supposed to be at my meeting. My first impulse is to tell Frank what I have discovered. He will immediately have Len arrested, and that would not be good enough for me. I have a very satisfying ending planned for this motherfucking son of a bitch. I am so angry I have to walk it off. God help anybody who pisses me off tonight. I have to leave; the desire to kick in his door and beat the shit out of him is growing stronger by the minute. When I get mad, I have to separate myself from the rest of the world. I am capable of extreme violence when I lose my temper.

I decide to go to the Fraser River for a walk. When I was young, I used to go there to smoke pot and drink beer, with Bob and some other friends. Thinking of the past and how innocent we were calms me down. I am able to think more clearly.

How did Randy and his dad become involved with these guys? Are they part of it—or is it just coincidence? I have more questions than answers, but I know some answers are on the way. I entered into all this because I wanted to punish the people who murdered Louisa, and the drug dealers. It has quickly become much more. Why am I surprised? Drugs bring out the worst in people. The need for getting a fix overcomes all morality, bringing out depravity. It seems I am about to enter a world where goodness is nonexistent. Heroin and cocaine, the worst drugs in the world, seem to be at the heart of everything. Rape and murder are two other things that seem to be associated with this bunch of people.

Calmed down, I head home. When I get there, Frank is inside waiting for me. Good thing I've taken time to calm down. He knows me so well he would know something has come up. One thing about being a drug addict—you become a good actor. How else can you hide what you really are from the rest of the world?

«Hi, brought you the videos. They are sorted with the names of the people in them written on the outside. I would stay and help out, but I have some business to take care of,» Frank explains.

«Okay,» I say. «One thing before you go. Who was the guy you brought to the hospital that day? I think his name was Ken.»

«That's Amy's uncle. He just wanted to come by and see

who you were and try to convey his good wishes, without telling you who he was. He wanted to offer you a job, but because of the circumstances he could not,» Frank says, looking at me.

«Okay, tell him I know everything now, and tell him the guy is getting what he deserves. I don't think I need a job, either.»

«Will do. I have to get going. See you tomorrow, or is Margaret coming over?»

«I hope so. I have a feeling I won't be letting her come by much longer. I think things might be getting dangerous soon,» I say.

«Something you need to tell me?» Frank asks.

«No,» I say, «just a feeling I've been getting. I think we are closing in on something, maybe a smuggling operation. There seems to be too much secrecy about that supply room at work. The two sleaze bags I've met so far seem very suspicious.

«By the way, what was the name of the guy who drugged Amy?» I ask.

«His name? It was Bruce something. Don't remember his last name. The video is in the pile. Actually there are two or three. The apartment address is written also. Okay, gotta go,» he says.

Closing the door behind him, I look at the stack of videos. God, I can't look at these tonight. I just got calmed down. Knowing I won't sleep, I take a sleeping pill, which I hate to do, as I don't feel rested in the morning. I cannot think about this jerk anymore tonight. With thoughts of what I have in mind for him (and for anybody else I find) brings a smile to my face as I fall asleep.

The next morning at work, I wander over to the supply room. I still have to get a couple of cameras in here. But first things first—Len's apartment is next. I only have four or five left. Hope it will be enough. I ask Len for a few items, barely stopping myself from smashing his face in. Now I know what they mean. Revenge is a dish best served cold. The anticipation of the first blow to his face is a real turn on, almost sexual in nature. I ask him what he's doing for lunch.

«Gotta do inventory,» he says. «Why?» he asks.

«Was going to ask you if you wanted to go for lunch, get to know you a bit better,» I say casually. «Guess I'll go to a meeting instead.»

«Maybe another time,» he says.

That worked out pretty good, but to be on the safe side I ask him, «What is your favourite pizza?»

«Ham and pineapple.»

«Well, I'm going to order a couple. You guys can split it, but save me half of one. I won't have time to eat if I go to a meeting,» I say.

«Hey thanks. That will be better than the lunch I brought.»

Thinking I have done all I can to keep him at work, I go to my bench and do a few little jobs while constantly looking at the clock. It's like I'm waiting for my connection to arrive. The anticipation is overwhelming. Almost as good as getting high. I have to stop thinking that way.

Arriving at the apartment, I see a sign on the front lawn that was not there yesterday, «apartment for sale.» Oh good, maybe there's no manager to look out for. I know there is no buzzer to get in. I go to the apartment door wondering what the best way to get in would be. I see on the doorframe by the lock that somebody has already pried the door open before. I have brought a couple of screwdrivers with me. This is too easy. The first screwdriver fits exactly in the groove that was there before. I find the end of the catch, and it slides easily open. Going in, I recognize the place. The furniture is even the same. I look around. It's surprisingly clean. I check out the rooms—there are two bedrooms separated by a bathroom. The first room is furnished, but no blankets are on the bed, and a layer of dust is on things. Bruce's room?

I look in the other bedroom, fully furnished with an unmade king-size bed. I see a pot pipe on the dresser, smell it, and the unmistakable odour of coke is in it. Oh no, hope this does not fuck me up. I look in his night table and see some syringes and a couple of flaps that look very full. I start to reach for them, temptation rearing its ugly head. Slowly I remove my hand, slide the drawer shut, looking wistfully at it the whole time. I stand there a minute or two, the hold this has on me almost overwhelming.

I finally come back to earth thinking, That's not why I'm here. Breathing a sigh of relief, I go to the final room. On the outside it looks ordinary. As I push the door open, I notice it's made of metal with two deadbolts top and bottom. I walk in and see the walls are very thick. Man, this place is soundproof. I see a lot of equipment. Most are things that are used to constrain a person in different positions.

What a sick fuck this guy is. There are handcuffs, shackles, whips, assorted gags, and blindfolds. There are even hoods with extra padding over the ears and straps going under the chin to hold the mouth closed. Feeling sick, I start planting the cameras, one for each wall. They are easy to hide, as he has hooks and eyelets all over them. I have one left. He has a phone by the sofa, so I decide to put the last one near it.

I notice in his room a set of keys on the dresser. I go back in, my eyes moving to the drawer. If you take it, he'll know someone has been here. Besides, it's not for you anymore.

I grab the keys, checking the locks on the torture room as I think of it. One of the keys fit. I try the other one in the front door, and it fits.

I go to the bathroom, look in the cupboard. There is a bunch of bars of soap. Hopefully he won't miss one bar. I soak the bar in water to soften it up and make impressions of the keys. I let it harden again and put it in the wrapper. So far an hour has passed. I glance around the room to see if I have left a trace of my presence. Satisfied, I leave.

This is going to be one place I will look at every day, and nobody else is going to know about it. On the way back to work, I stop by the hardware store and buy six key blanks, extras in case I screw some up.

Back at work, the excitement is gone, but the fact that I did not use is a very satisfying feeling. I start making the keys. I make a pattern on some cardboard and cut it out. As I'm filing the blanks, Len comes up with a pizza box.

He hands it to me and asks, «What's the key for?»

«Oh, my apartment. They only gave me one key, and I like a few extras, always losing them,» I reply. There is something really satisfying making the keys right in front of him. He's watching his own demise and does not even know it.

After work, I go home and turn the computer on. Nothing is happening yet. Len has not come back. I make some coffee, and just as I finish pouring a cup, I hear a door slam. The sound is on the computer, and Len is walking into the room. I hear a knock on his door; Len walks over and opens it. On the other side is someone I knew too well, Art. It feels like my heart has stopped beating. Hatred comes over me in waves.

I hear Len say, «Hi bro, come on in.»

I look at the both of them; they look different but the same. You can tell they are related. Now I know why I could not quite place Len. Art is Len's brother.

Art is saying, «Just came by to see when I can move my stuff in. Can't wait to use that room over there again.» He points to the room with all the torture devices.

Len says, «Anytime, here's a key.»

Chapter 15

This is great. I don't even have to look for the creep. He's already in my sights. We sure made the right decision in my coming back to work here. The pieces are starting to fit.

I can't believe myself. I had totally forgotten about Art. Even though there was so much going on, how could I forget about one of the pricks who killed Louisa? I have to plan this carefully. This guy is going to die, and believe me, it will be traumatic. Lost in thought, I realize I have not been listening to the conversation.

Art is telling Len, «I'll move a few things in tonight and the rest while you are at work tomorrow. I want to get some things in place. I have some plans for the room tomorrow. Can you be somewhere else tomorrow night?»

«No sweat,» says Len.

«A shipment is arriving in two days, and I have to move things around at work and deliver whats still there tomorrow night. It's going to be a big payday.»

«Great, I have a couple of people coming over for a training session,» Art brags.

«Okay. Don't worry about the noise—it's really well soundproofed,» Len tells Art.

«Yeah, I know. Me and Bruce have used it many times already,» Art says. «Oh, I heard some things about Bruce the other day. They've been giving him hormones, and they tattooed his lips a bright red. A little Vaseline on them and it looks like lipstick. They have halter pants on him, as they won't let him wear a dress. There have been arguments on how much hormone to give him. Some of the guys like small firm breasts. Others want them big. Fuck, if I was him I'd kill myself somehow.» Len is grinning widely as he is saying this.

«He always was a coward. He always needed to be high when we were doing something a little scary. Made me do all the rough stuff. Prick deserves it for getting caught. I hated having to work with him. He was good at the sex stuff, although a real pervert.»

«Well he's getting all the perversion he can handle now. Wish I could see it,» says Len. «Louise would love it.»

The name Louise brings me up short. Is it Mark's wife?

«Yeah, she would. She is coming over tomorrow with a new girl, going to start the training. The first time she will be doing the whipping and stuff. Louise likes that sometimes, likes to watch,» Art says.

That gives me time to plan. I'll stay in tomorrow night, see who's who. I'm already pretty sure what I am going to do to Art. The thought almost makes the wait worthwhile. I know I won't be able to sleep again tonight, so I take another sleeping pill. Anticipating the next two days is going to be a very good feeling.

At work the next day, feeling groggy because of the sleeping pill, I am almost cheerful. I wave at Len with a grin on my face.

«Hey, come over here, Chris,» he says.

Walking over, I say hi to Gord, the spray man. I start to walk away, thinking, Gord or Gordon? He was a meek and mild kind of guy, almost subservient in a way. He grew up with my boss, and they've worked together forever. Is he the Gord I'm looking for, Gordon? Have I stumbled onto something here? Looking very thoughtful, I walk over to Len.

He tells me, «I am going to be busy the next couple of days, maybe going to Vancouver Island. I might be gone a day or two, so grab what you need now.»

«Okay,» I say. «I'll make a list—be right back.» I go look over the jobs needing to be done. I guess what's needed, double it just in case. I give the list to him.

«Give me half an hour,» he tells me.

On the way back to my workbench I stop off to talk with Gord. «Hey man, sorry we have not talked since I've been back, but I had no real opportunity. Len is getting me some supplies, so not much to do at the moment. How have you been?»

«Okay,» he says, not looking at me, but that's not that unusual for him. He rarely looks a person in the eyes, and then only briefly. «Just working, you know, and a little booze now and then,» he informs me. I can't tell by his attitude if he has something to be guilty about. He seems the same. Anyway, I'll be keeping an eye on him.

«Okay,» I say. «See ya.»

Len waves at me. The supplies are ready.

«I've been asking around about you. They say you get pretty fucked up at times but always manage to clean up. When you do, you are a pretty decent guy. Maybe when I get back, let's see if we can get to know each other,» Len suggests.

With a big grin I say, «Sure, that's been exactly what I've been thinking. We can have a friendly little chat.» With you hanging by your wrists, a gag in your mouth, and nice little whip marks all over your scrawny, little body. «Can hardly wait.»

With another grin at him I go back to my bench with the cart of stuff, rearrange my bench to accommodate it all, and go to work. Happily the day goes by fast. I go to see Len, just to make sure he's still going to be staying late.

I ask him, «You going to be here awhile? Want me to put some coffee on?»

«Yeah man, that would be great. Going to be here for hours and hours. I have a mattress here, and I'm going to sleep a bit and then work some more.»

Going over to the coffee pot, after resisting the urge to spit into it, I make him some coffee. Then I yell over to him saying, «Coffee is on. Enjoy, and don't work too hard.» This is exactly what I want. He's away from his apartment, but I know where he will be.

«I never do,» he says.

And soon, never again.

Chapter 16

B ack at home, I move the computer to where I can see it
from the kitchen. I start making something to eat. I see
Art moving things in, boxes and a few pieces of furniture.
He goes into the room where all the equipment is stored. For
an hour or so I watch him arranging the things he wants to
use—the whips, gags, leather hood, an electric horse prod,
and something like leather shoelaces. Man, what will they
think of next?

He is doing all this with a great air of excitement. Finally
the bell rings, and there she is—Mark's wife, Louise. I stare
at her. I don't know if I should hate her or not. She walks
into the room, slaps Art across the face with the back of her
hand. It must have hurt a lot. He immediately falls to his
knees, his head bowed. This really surprises me. I thought he
was the dominant one. Suddenly I like Louise a bit more.

Louise tells him to «strip and put the ball gag on.» He
immediately starts to get up to strip, and she says, «On your
knees, prick.»

«Yes, mistress.»

After he is naked, he crawls to the other room, Louise
following him. «I am going to put this on video so you can
watch it later.»

She gets a camera and tapes him putting the ball gag
on. There is a chain fixed to the ceiling, the eyelet made

of shiny steel with a steel collar on the other end. «Put on the manacles at your feet!» They are about two-and-a-half feet apart. After he does this, he looks very unbalanced and uncomfortable. «Put the collar on. Lock it with the padlock. Put the harness around your waist and shoulders, nice and tight, and lock it with the padlock. Now shackle your hands in the manacles.» He complies without hesitation. She stops the camera and puts it down.

«Be right back, prick. There is someone at the door. On second thought—» She turns the camera back on, points it at him, and says, «Put the chain around the manacles so your hands are forced together. Move your arms up and down.» His arms can only move up and down for three or four inches starting from just below his waist. Satisfied, she turns the camera off and leaves the room.

She goes to the door, and a girl is there. Louise says, «He's ready. Are you?»

«Oh yes,» says the girl, something familiar about the voice, but I cannot see her face. I have to fix the position of the camera.

Louise takes her arm and leads her into the bathroom where I don't have a camera, only a microphone. I still have not had a look at her face. «Stay here and change. There is a hood so your face will be hidden. I don't want him freaking if he gets to see your face. Take your clothes off, and put these on. They are rubber, and the blood will wash off. Don't touch anything until you have the gloves on. I'll change in the other room.» The door opens, and Louise walks out.

I am sitting in my living room by now, and I am amazed that Art could make himself as helpless as this. He really is a sick individual. I had heard stories about this BDSM, but still could not believe my eyes. To need to feel humiliated and made to be helpless, what the fuck?

When I was high I was helpless, but you are not aware of the helplessness, nor would you care. Art was a guy that I knew liked life a bit. I had heard him laugh, and he had sex, even though it was rape. I had thought him to be perverted but aggressive. I had to see more of this. I was wishing I was there doing horrible things to him.

Louise calls out to the girl, «You ready yet?»

«Yes, just waiting for you.» She comes out the door dressed all in shiny black, covered head to foot. So is Louise. They go into the room where Art is. Louise sets the camera at an angle so it can record Art's every movement. Very little of the girls is seen. They stand looking at Art. He is standing in the middle of the room, a collar and chain around his neck, hands manacled in front of him, and legs spread apart. What an idiot.

«This is a video-only camera. The audio has been turned off,» she says to the girl. «Hey prick, this is my new slave, and I am going to instruct her in the finer points of BDSM tonight. Her name is Candy.»

Art is bound, helpless and with the ball gag cannot talk, except make a deep, almost gagging sound. Louise walks over to the items Art picked out. They are all his favourites. «Me and prick here have done this many times. He likes it very much. Don't you, prick?» Art nods his head.

She picks up the leather thongs and tells Candy they are to bind the balls and his penis. «I'll do this. If it's too tight, the circulation will be cut off, and he will lose his prick and his balls.» She bends over, showing Candy how it is done.

She gives Art a snort of something. «To heighten the experience,» she tells Candy. «Now pick up the whip and hit him, gradually hitting harder and harder.» Candy picks up the whip and starts to hit him with enthusiasm. Louise puts earplugs in Art's ears.

«Have you done this before?» Louise asks.

«No, but you know how much I hate him. I am enjoying this already. Thanks, Louise. You are such a good friend.»

«Well, I heard what he and Bruce did to you, much as he did to me. Art was Bruce's little plaything; but since he is in jail, I do this to Art now. I hate him as much as you. Keep going. Hit him everywhere, even the balls,» Louise orders.

Hearing this, my heart goes out to them both, for I finally realize who Candy is—Amy.

«God, you've got courage, girl,» I say to myself.

«Hit him harder for a few more minutes. See, he is getting a hard on and is playing with himself. I'll tighten the thongs some more in a bit,» Louise coaches.

«Now take the cattle prod and turn it up. Get him everywhere after I tighten the thongs. After that we will kill him.»

«Oh great, I have been dreaming of this day for months,» Amy says.

Hearing this, I know I have to get over there—now. I can't let Amy and Louise have this on their conscience. It's about a ten-minute walk to Len's. I make it in five. I use my key to open the front door, walk in, rush to the bondage room, open that door, and walk in. Amy is using the cattle prod on him, and it is turned to high now. Art is masturbating furiously. Both women turn and look at me and gasp.

«Chris,» both of them say at once.

«Turn the camera off,» I tell them. Louise goes to the camera, carefully avoiding being seen by the camera. Art, oblivious to my presence, continues to masturbate. It is the last picture on the camera. «I know you are upset and surprised by my arrival tonight, but this is one of the pricks that killed Louisa. Bill was the other one. Art was just along for the ride I think.»

I walk over to him and kick him in the nuts. The noises coming from behind the ball gag are very satisfying to hear.

«I need you both to go, not another word until I see you both tomorrow at my apartment. Frank knows the address. Tomorrow after five we'll have dinner. Now go change.»

They hesitate, and I say, «Don't worry. Art will be dealt with, okay?» They nod, go get changed, and leave.

After they are gone, I lock the door, look around to see if anything is out of place. I wipe down anything I think the girls might have touched. I do not really worry about mine too much. I can say they were from when I was here the last time.

I walk over to Art and knock him out. I tighten the thongs around his balls and penis so that there is no chance in hell they are going to survive. I make a loop on the end of one of them, catching it onto the handcuffs, making it look like he had tightened the thong himself. I had read that was how they gelded horses. I wait about an hour, knocking him out one more time before I allow him to wake up. I take his earplugs out and come around so he can see me. A look of terror comes over his face.

«Remember me? What was it Louise called you? Oh yeah, prick.»

I proceeded to do things to him that hurt but do not leave marks, the cattle prod being used the most, as it leaves no trace. His balls and penis, not knowing they are dead yet, still feel pain. I get a mirror and place it where he can see his penis. He can barely move by now. I tell him he can hang himself very easily if he cannot live without his cock and balls.

I explain what I have done to his privates, and he looks so horrified it will live pleasantly in my memory forever.

He looks in the mirror, sees his penis has turned almost black, and starts touching it. I turn the camera back on. He is rubbing it so hard it looks like he is still masturbating. He tries to take the binding off but does not have the strength. I sit down and watch him.

It takes about five hours, his penis obviously dead, his balls a very pretty shade indeed. He looks at me and with defeat and shock lets his body go limp, and hangs himself.

I quietly get up and leave, no hint of my presence anywhere.

CHAPTER 17

O n the way home my spirits are very high. Both of the people who actually killed Louisa are now dealt with. Now to find out who hired them, and why? That is still important to me.

I do not think Art's death will bring much attention. The video clearly shows him doing it to himself. He was such an asshole his record must be a mile long. The cops will likely say good riddance to bad rubbish. It's going to be another sleeping pill night I think. The trouble with sleeping pills is you don't dream, or at least I don't. Dreams are nature's way of getting rid of the stress of everyday living. You take them long enough, you start acting and thinking strange thoughts.

Anyway, got to work tomorrow, so I can't risk anything suspicious. It's already late. He won't be discovered for a day or two at least. I get to my apartment and open the door. Frank, Amy, and Louise are there. Oh fuck, what's up here?

«Hi, Chris, we've got some serious talking to do here. You know everybody, so I guess we can get right down to it. What happened after the girls left?»

«Well, Art has repented for his sins and killed himself. I did not really try to stop him. He got almost what he deserved,» I say as reasonably as I can.

«I guess you're wondering if I am going to arrest you now. Well, I'm not. Amy, Louise, and I have been planning this little scenario for months. Bruce, Art, and once in a while Len have done to about fifty other girls what they did to Amy. Maybe it was even more than that. He was especially horrible to Louise. Amy and Louise met at Len's and became friends.

«When you appeared on the scene to rescue Amy, they had already swapped stories and had come to me with it. When you and Margaret overheard those guys at the treatment center, I knew what had to be done,» Frank explains. «But you seemed to get there a little bit ahead of us. On almost everything, it seems, even with your record of getting stoned. Very impressive, and you're not even trained.»

«Well, when you do drugs you get paranoid and start looking at everything you need to in order to stay alive,» I tell him.

«What's the plan now? Art's last moments were very painful,» Frank states.

«Oh,» I say, looking at the computer. «You saw?»

«Yes, everything. He got what he deserved. I almost went into vice because of assholes like Art, but it would have destroyed me as a person. The sick things people do to one another. Man, you look exhausted. But before you go to sleep, erase this from your computer. It will be our secret. I have to protect Amy, and Louise since she has been helping Amy a lot, and they don't need any more grief.»

I tell Frank, «Art won't be found for a while, as Len is working on deliveries and incoming shipments and won't be home for a day or two.»

As he is leaving, Frank tells me, «The police are going to raid Len's apartment tomorrow. When Bob found out that Art was moving in, they issued the warrant. He has had one out on him for a while now because of his involvement with Bruce. It is probably better this way. Len won't be able to change what happened there. He would probably try to hide it to keep the cops out of his business. I want you to stay home tomorrow, as the warrant also includes his place of work.»

«I think you are going to find some things there. He is expecting a shipment tomorrow and is working there tonight. He's making room and arranging what is already there,» I inform Frank.

«I wonder when that shipment is going to arrive. We'll arrange to serve the warrant as it is being unloaded. Now I've got to make a phone call and get them to change the plan. Thanks,» he says.

«Not a problem, you know we have to talk more about this, don't you?» I ask him.

«Yeah, I know, but don't worry. You only did what I was going to do. I was going to bring you into the picture, but Art's moving into Len's speeded things up. The window of opportunity opened sooner than we thought it would. Sorry,» he says.

«Okay. I just had to get there so they would not have to carry around any guilt.»

«I understand,» Frank says. «Just don't ever get mad at me,» he grins. «Okay, I have to leave now.»

The girls are listening to all this, not saying a word. They get up, run to Frank and hug him. Louise says, «Thanks, Frank. We both are grateful to you and to Chris. We'll talk to you soon.»

«All right,» he says. «Bye until then.» He goes out the door.

«Well, girls, you want anything before we talk a bit—coffee? I'm making some anyway.»

«Sure,» they say at the same time.

Louise says, «It's been a long time, Chris, ever since

Mark and I broke up.»

«You broke up when?» I ask her.

«A couple of months before Louisa was killed. I'm so sorry, Chris. I really liked her.»

Has it been that long? Was I so fucked up that I could not recall the last time we saw each other? Yes, I guess it was. We were not very close because Mark and Louise were into heroin. The lifestyle of heroin users is a dangerous place to be. The withdrawal from heroin is a very hard thing to endure, and an addict will do anything not to face it. Cocaine users, since the quality of coke is changing, are fast approaching the heroin lifestyle. Robbery, muggings, bank robbery, and even murder are all on the list.

For women, I'm sorry to say, prostitution is their way of life. Mark, I'm afraid to say, was involved in some of these activities. I'm not sure which ones, and I really don't want to know.

I ask her, «Do you see Mark around at all? I have not seen him since the funeral.»

«No, he travels in different circles now. He got involved in heroin and coke and was using both of them. I think he started to owe a lot of money.»

There it is again, heroin and coke. I'm thinking it is mainly one or two people who are at the center of it. One of them is responsible for Louisa's death. The girls are quiet, seeing I am deep in thought. I hear the kettle boiling, get up and make the coffee. The action takes me back to the here and now.

«Do you know any of these dealers, Louise?» I ask her.

«I know a few of the smaller ones. I knew a Randy. I went out with him for a while, well actually just sex and drugs. I did not get to know him at all. I don't know much about him. He kept his personal things hidden from me. Do the drugs, have sex, and leave—that kind of guy.»

«What does he look like?» I ask her. She describes a person that sounds like Randy at work.

«He bought a brand new Jeep a while ago,» she says.

«Oh fuck, I know him. I work for his dad.»

CHAPTER 18

We talked a little for a while, but not about what had just happened. I was still out of it. In times of stress or any other strong emotion, I get physically drained. It's as if I use all my stored up energy. After the rush is over, I get tired and can't think straight. It has been this way ever since I can remember.

I ask the girls, «Do you want to sleep in the bedroom? I'll sleep on the couch.»

«Sure,» they agree, as it is getting late. «We're feeling a little weird over what happened tonight.» I figure they want to talk about it themselves.

I tell them, «The place is yours, food and whatever else you need. There are extra toothbrushes in the drawer in the bathroom.» I lie down on the couch and am asleep in minutes. I sleep about four hours, waking up to the smell of coffee, bacon, eggs, and toast.

«After I eat, I am going to work. This is something I can't miss. I've been planting cameras for what seems like forever and have witnessed only one arrest, Bruce's. I really want to see more.»

«Thanks for the breakfast. I'm going to work, so talk to you later,» I tell them.

«Sure, thanks for last night. You were right. We might be feeling really guilty right now if you had not come over.

Okay, talk with you soon. Go enjoy yourself,» Amy says with a big grin.

I find I cannot work properly, finding it hard not to look and act excited. I am really looking forward to this. I walk over to Len, who looks very tired. «How you doing?» I ask him.

«Tired, was going to have to have a bit of sleep, but the supplies will be arriving in a few minutes.»

«Yeah, I'm tired too. Not getting enough sleep myself.» I find a place to sit where I can see everything that will be happening all around me. A truck arrives with a Washington license plate. The driver walks over to Len and says, «Where do you want it, Len?» slapping him on the back in a friendly way.

«In the usual place. I cleaned it out last night,» Len tells him. The driver goes back to the truck, opens the doors, and is carrying the first pail out when the cops arrive.

«Man oh man, there's cops everywhere,» says Len. «This is bad, oh so fucking bad.»

I know we have him. The excitement in me is building.

Len is looking around as if to see where he can run. The cops are covering every exit, and there are at least twenty officers. Guns drawn, they scatter all over the shop. On TV you see the police come in one or two doors, giving the bad guys the opportunity to grab a gun. In the show a big fight ensues, guns going off, fists flying, and the bad guys dropping. This raid is nothing like that. The cops are everywhere all at once. Nobody has a chance to do anything.

An addict has a strong survival instinct, protecting only their drugs. They are very selfish and will not risk injury. The cops round us all up, take us to the lunchroom, searching each of us before going in. They leave four cops to guard us, fear in a lot of eyes. Some of them drug addicts, they know they're in for a bad few days. Withdrawal in custody is a very unpleasant thing.

I sit next to Len just to feel his fear. Just then Frank walks in. Len looks at him. He looks at me, and I see something in his eyes that I don't like. «We found lots of drugs. You guys are all going to jail,» Frank tells us. He looks at each one of us as if to memorize our faces. When it's my turn, I see the anger in his eyes. On the way out of the lunchroom we all get handcuffed. When Frank gets to me, he gives the cuffs an extra squeeze and says to me, «Have a good day, idiots.» I know it is meant for me.

Len is watching us, and I know he has made some connection between Frank and me. I don't know what has made him suspicious, but he is. I decide not to let him out of my sight. I know Len is on to me, and I won't let him spread the news.

We are led to a couple of paddy wagons. Frank has a few words with everyone. When he gets to me, he says, «I told you to stay at home today. You're really pissing me off.»

«I think Len knows we are somehow connected. He looked at you, then me, and a thoughtful, angry look came on his face,» I whisper to Frank.

Strange as this may sound, I have never been in a paddy wagon, or for that matter, in a jail cell. At the police station we are all put in a big cell. I know it will be a long wait, as they want the addicts to start withdrawing before they get questioned. They will be more willing to talk. Len keeps trying to stay away from me, but it is not easy, as I keep moving with him. This is going to be interesting.

When I first started all this, I never thought about bravery. Was I or wasn't I? It did not matter. When I get angry, I think I can do just about anything and often do. I find myself looking forward to what I know is going to come.

Len is pretty strong. He moves barrels and other heavy

things around all day. But he has a big belly and smokes, gets winded easily. I'm pretty strong myself and know how to take care of myself. I also have another advantage. When I'm in a fight, I don't feel any pain. I get so angry pain cannot find its way in. By now I know a fight is going to happen, to the death maybe?

Len's death? I find myself looking forward to it, but first I have to make sure he does not talk with anyone. Len finally sits down. I make the guy next to him move, and I take his place. Len starts to get up. I grab his arm and keep him where he is.

«What's wrong, Len, you afraid of something?» I ask innocently.

«Nope, just found out I don't like you much, rat,» he says.

«What do you mean, Len, you know all about me?»

«I saw that cop coming out of your building, from your apartment,» he says.

«Which cop? What's going on here? Have you got the cops looking at me? You sure he was in my apartment?» I ask, acting surprised.

«Yes. The one who told us we were going to jail,» he says. «I know you're the one responsible for all this shit today.

«If you got them looking at me, I'm gonna beat the shit out of you,» I counter.

«I haven't done anything to you,» Len says, suddenly afraid.

«All the time I've been doing and selling drugs did I have cops nosing around? Not once! I'm smarter than that,» I tell him, looking pissed off. Now I know it was a good idea to come to work today. Hopefully, I have lessened his suspicion of me. «If I get any hassle from this I'm gonna come for you. You can count on it,» I tell him in an angry whisper.

«I'm sorry if I did, but I still don't trust you,» he says.

«You know, I don't give a shit what you think. It's what I think that should matter to you. I don't let anyone mess with me,» I say in the most threatening way I can.

«Well, time will tell, Chris. Time will tell.»

I think I've handled it pretty well considering I'd not had much time to make all this up. He still does not know about his brother, and I think when he does know his mind will not be on me. Just then an officer calls my name. I have to go talk with somebody. A cop leads me away.

«Be cool,» I say to Len.

«In here, you bet. It's too dangerous not to be.»

«Frank wants to interview you. This way,» says the cop.

«Not much choice there, I guess?» I ask the cop.

«No, none at all,» he says. When I get to the room, the cop takes the cuffs off and says, «He'll be a couple of minutes.»

«Okay. Thanks,» I reply.

When Frank comes in, I tell him what Len and I had said. I tell Frank when Len is told about Art, and how he died, he will not be thinking about me anymore. «Give me five minutes, and then come release me if you can. I don't like it here.»

«Not many do,» he says. «But I should let you sit here for a while because you pissed me off. I guess it turned out for the best. Okay, you'll get your five minutes.» He rings for the cop to take me back. «Bring Len in after ten minutes or so. I've got some writing to do before I'm ready for him,» he tells the other cop.

After the cop brings me back to the cell, I walk over to Len, who is still sitting where I left him. «You fucking asshole,» I yell and punch him in the face, aiming six inches past it, the way I had been taught. He falls back on the floor, tries to stand, stumbles, regains his balance, and comes after me. I let him get close. As he is swinging his arm to punch me, I knee him in the balls. When he doubles over, I give him a black eye with my knee. Just then two cops come in to take me away. Two more are there helping Len to his feet. They take him out of the cell and get him a cold, wet towel to wipe the blood away and help reduce the swelling. They take him to the room where Frank is.

About three or four minutes later I hear a scream. «Oh no, not Art!» It's Len's voice.

«Sounds like he got some bad news,» I say to no one in particular.

«Yeah, his brother killed himself after he had a slight accident.»

Awww isn't that a fucking shame!

CHAPTER 19

Once I am released from the jail, I go home, make some coffee, and crash on the couch. Reflecting on the past few days, it is amazing to me how much I actually hate these people. I get angry just thinking about all the lives they have destroyed for power and money. I also hate that I have been involved in it myself in the past.

Why do I feel no guilt for what I have done lately? Come to think of it, fuck them. Those guys deserved what I did to them. No one else seems to be doing much to stop them. With all the money and with the people they can buy, they are almost unstoppable. It's amazing the people who are caught up in drugs. Anybody, and I mean anybody, can get addicted. With addiction comes debt, with debt comes obligation, and with obligation comes slavery. You are forced to do what your dealer wants. You do it and while doing it, you hate it. All that is forgotten as soon as you get high again. It goes round and round. The only way to stop is to quit using. Some drugs are so powerful it's almost impossible to stop. The pressure from your dealer and the people you use with make it even harder.

When I went into treatment, I had to cut all ties. I usually owed my dealer money. One thing though—when I did clean up, I never did pay back the money I owed, sometimes in the thousands. What's even funnier is they never tried to collect, not one of them. I could never understand why. Maybe they respected what I was doing; they knew how hard it is to quit. They knew firsthand how hard it is. Maybe they knew that the fear of not being able to score was not there anymore, that I was not afraid of them.

To be an addict is to stop developing emotionally, morally, and spiritually. You learn no social skills, have no friends, and do not even want them. You do learn how to lie, cheat, and steal.

I'm thinking of my brother. Where is he? I have no clue how to find him. I know none of his friends or if he even has any. I need to talk with Louise. Is she right? Did he owe money? Was he the reason for the hit on Louise, a warning to him to pay what he owed? I do not know, but I'm going to try to find out.

Frank is also on my mind. I'm still surprised by his actions concerning Art. Being an undercover officer, he must have seen the very worst in people. I am surprised that more cops do not have a vengeful attitude. Maybe they do. I would not really be surprised. I decide I have to see Frank, talk to him about Len and how he reacted. The scream I heard at the police station was the first thing I would ask about.

I will walk over to Len's and see what's up there. Tomorrow I will go and see what is going on at work, unless it's closed. It takes me fifteen minutes to get to Len's, walking slowly and thinking. I want to use Len's apartment and maybe his bondage equipment. There are all sorts of equipment I do not know the purpose of.

I see no evidence of police in the area, so I decide to go inside. There is a yellow ribbon, but it does not say crime scene. They must have decided not to pursue the matter. I open the door, and it's like I left it, except there is no Art.

I still feel no guilt. He deserved it. The only problem with the whole revenge thing is that I might start to enjoy it. The rush was overwhelming, a high itself. Got to focus on it, being a necessity for my peace of mind. Vengeance for those he molested and the ones he can no longer harm. The other room is not as I left it. The police have obviously examined every piece of equipment, and they were not really careful where they threw it.

A new thought comes to me. I will get Len to lease this apartment to me. His brother died here. Would he want to live here? I'll have to approach him carefully, let him know somehow that I'm interested in bondage. The plan seems entirely plausible to me. I can be very persuasive if I need to be. Maybe I'll start talking to Len about the dangers involved in that lifestyle, say I want to learn. Yeah, it will work. I'll make it work.

I head home to look at Bruce's computers. When I get home, I discover that I cannot access his files. They are password protected. Maybe my friend who owns the spy store has a program to open them. Instead, I watch some of the videos. What I am seeing is very depraved, worse than what happened to Amy. There are at least four other men involved that I don't know. Sickened, I turn it off.

I'm going to do something about this, but I have some unfinished business to take care of first.

Another sleeping pill night I'm afraid. No, I've been relying on them too much.

I'm going to call Margaret. Being with that beautiful woman will be better than any pill. When I call, she is almost out the door before hanging up. I put all the videos away. I'm slow and gentle with Margaret, tender, lots of kissing, gentle caresses. I go to sleep lying on top of her, still inside her. She wakes me after a few minutes and rolls me off. «It feels good, but you were getting too heavy,» she whispers in my ear.

I drift back to sleep. When I wake up, it's noon. The coffee just needs to be turned on, bread in the toaster, eggs whipped for scrambled eggs. Her note says, «You needed the sleep, see you later, love you, Marg.»

After eating, I decide to go to work and see what's up. There are still a lot of cops around, mostly lab techs going over everything. There are none of my co-workers around. I see Frank and walk over.

«We found a lot of heroin and coke ready for shipment, but at first did not find any in the new shipment. Almost all the containers had been opened at that point. Two officers were opening different five-gallon drums, got sloppy, and splashed the contents of one drum onto the other. It immediately started bubbling. After a few minutes the liquid disappeared, leaving a white powder. It tested as almost pure cocaine. So, they put some of the other liquid into another container with the same result. This time it turned out to be almost pure heroin. The drums were from Washington,» Frank explains to me.

I walk over for a closer look—lots of containers. Frank talks some more: «These containers are a new type, designed to be safer in transport. A few years back a truckload of these products, in a different type of container, caught on fire and exploded. Did a lot of damage and injured a bunch of people. They are essentially two containers in one, a white non-flammable substance cushioning the contents. The substance has been replaced with cocaine and heroin and somehow hardened. We have not found out how they do it yet, but now we know how it is being brought in. This is going to be huge,»

Frank continues to explain. «The dogs could not even smell it because of the chemical inside. A very clever smuggling ring behind this. We can trace the origin of the drums and find out who they are.

«We owe you a lot for this find, Chris.

Chapter 20

On the way home, I go over the things I have accomplished in these past few months: Bill is dead, Bruce is unhappy in jail, Art is dead by his own hand. I cannot be blamed for his death, that is, if all the video is actually erased from the computer. I'm sure I can trust Frank on that, and I'm almost positive Amy would not have let him keep it.

I smile, thinking about the drug dealers that have already been arrested, and the ones that are still being looked at. In addition, there is now this big bust with international connections. Who knows where that will lead? Mexico? Peru? Brazil? Columbia? Not bad for a drug addict like me. Maybe, in a twisted way, it was for the best that I was a drug addict. The good I have done perhaps is worth the pain and struggle. The loss of Louisa, however, is not an acceptable part. That is something nothing will heal. The world is not so bright with her not in it. My world especially.

My love for Margaret is so good and new. It is something that if taken from me as well, I surely will not survive.

What do I do from here? Somebody or something holds the key. Is it the videos or Bruce's computers?

I decide to take the computer to my friend, see if he can open the files. I am very reluctant to watch the videos, afraid of how they will make me feel. I know the anger and the need for vengeance will be overwhelming, the pity and remorse I will feel, just as bad.

Maybe I should embrace these emotions. Let them override the joy and excitement I feel when I am getting my revenge. That is something that has to stop. To feel that excitement and joy over somebody's agony is not acceptable. It makes me worse than them. Maybe the guilt I am feeling is the beginning of that cleansing. Even though they deserve punishment, it should be conducted with cold, calculating precision, not joy.

I take the computer to my friend. «I can't do it, but I know someone who can. It will cost you,» he informs me.

«Is he somebody you trust? There might be some pretty bad things on it,» I ask.

«Yes, I trust him, but it might take awhile. I'll call you.» I give him some money and plan to go home.

Instead, I go to the Alano Club just a couple of blocks west of Granville. There are meetings there and people who want company. I get a coffee and go on the balcony for a smoke. The guy I took for a coffee and gave some numbers to is there. He looks good, a little shaky, but good. «Hey, thought you were working,» he says.

«The place got busted yesterday, and there are still cops all over the place,» I tell him.

«Did they arrest Randy or Gord?» he asks.

«I don't know. Everyone was taken to the police station. From there I am not sure what happened. They let me go because I had just started working there. They said they'd be keeping an eye on me though.»

«Oh, well,» he says. «I won't be getting any more from them. I've decided to clean up, stay clean and sober. The numbers you gave me are for really nice people, really helpful.»

«Yeah. They helped me a lot also. Why do you mention Gord?»

«Well I had a friend who wanted a few ounces of coke and a bit of heroin, and I went to Randy. He told me to wait where I was. I watched him, and he went to talk with Gord. They walked off, and Randy came back with what I asked for. 'What does he want all this for? Randy asked, and I told him, 'He's having a party for a few rich guys.'»

«When was this?» I ask.

«A couple of months ago, I guess,» he says.

Gord is the quiet dude that will not look you in the eye. He keeps a low profile and lets others take the spotlight. He has never been friendly, stays in the background. Gonna find where he lives and check him out.

«I usually met Randy someplace else. But I thought the quantity I wanted might be hard to get, might take awhile. It surprised me that he had it there already.»

«Well, you definitely won't be getting it from there anymore. They might even close the business. The cops, I mean. Depends on whether Randy's dad was involved,» I surmise.

«I don't think so. I'm not sure, but Randy said he had to keep it from his dad. He already knew Randy was doing drugs. That's why he drinks so much. He did not know what to do to help.»

«Maybe that's why he hired me back,» I interrupted. «He knew I was clean and sober and could maybe help his son. Who knows? Well, keep up the good work. I gotta go now. Keep in contact with those guys, okay?» I tell him.

I should go to Randy's dad, find out what is happening. Maybe find out where Gord lives. Gonna need some more cameras. Was Gord the Gordon that Bill and Art were talking about?

I get to work. There are only a few lab techs there and one

or two officers to watch their backs. They are in the back, so I walk around to the front and see Randy's dad sitting with a drink in one hand and bottle in the other. He perks up a bit when he sees me, but the look lasts just a few seconds, and he returns to being dejected and looks pretty drunk.

Working on a computer in the corner is Randy's sister, Julie. I have not seen her in a long while. She is a very hot looking woman. I have never liked Julie; she is selfish and always making fun of her brother. She seems to know when Randy is feeling down. She will take him to lunch, get him drunk and high. She calls him, «my little pansy brother.» She looks at me and does not say a word, just goes back to the computer. Guess she does not like me, either.

«Hi Chris, glad to see they let you go. I told the officers you had just returned to work after a couple of years. You had no idea—I had no idea—what was going on right under my nose,» Randy's dad volunteers. «They arrested Randy. His prints were all over the drums that were already in the storage room. They're going to charge him with possession, dealing, and importing. What am I gonna do?»

«Well, getting drunk is not going to help him,» I lecture. «You need a clear head.»

«I went to the pub with Randy. He is doing a lot of drugs. If you really want to help him he's gotta go to treatment, stay clean and sober, and the judge might go easier on him. He's involved with something very big,» I suggest.

«That little pansy. He is such a weak little prick. Let him rot,» Julie says. «He will never quit drugs. He's too weak.»

«With a bitch like you around, no wonder,» I mutter under my breath.

She gets up, pours her dad a drink, and says, «Just like Dad, another weak pansy. See ya later,» as she goes out the door. Her dad gets red in the face and looks like he is about to cry. I remember her when I worked here before. She used to come by with a different guy on her arm all the time. They were usually rich. She kept showing us rings and other jewellery they would buy her. She kept losing the guys, saying they were fooling around on her. Jealous little bitch.

«Take it easy,» I say as she leaves.

«She probably just wants you to let Randy take care of his own problems,» I assure Randy's dad.

«Randy is still in jail. A bail hearing is set for tomorrow. I got a lawyer for him who says it's going to cost a lot of money. I'm going to make him sell his Jeep. He has some savings also, but I guess I will have to pay the rest. He will be out tomorrow. They let Gord go also. His fingerprints were nowhere to be found except in the shop. Len is screwed, going to be doing a lot of years. I'd better not see his face again. I had hoped with you back you could help Randy. I was going to talk to you at the beginning of next week. I wanted you to get used to being back at work, first,» he explains.

«Did you know that some of your employees were doing drugs?» I ask.

«No, I hardly go in the back now—what with my drinking and with Randy and Gord back there to keep an eye on things.»

«Are they going to close you down?» I ask.

«I don't know. That's why Julie was here going over who has received what. All the supplies were confiscated, and a lot of shops are not going to get theirs. I have to find out which shops got what and which shops still need to get theirs. She was printing out the phone numbers.»

I go over to the computer. It is still on. The phone list and delivery folder are on the screen, I open the folder. «She did not print it. Do you want me to do it for you?» I ask.

«Sure,» he says. I print two copies. I look at him, and he is looking out the window. I slip one copy into my pocket and put the other on his desk.

«Here you go. I have to go now. Take it easy on the booze. You can't help him if you're too drunk.»

Chapter 21

Outside I glance at the list, and there are a few companies that I know. Mike used to go to some of them. He knew people who worked there. Got to give this to Frank, show him the ones I know. With this list, it should be easy for them to find others who were receiving the drugs. I can see lots of search warrants served in the future.

So, Mike is back in the picture, even though he's dead. Man, the wreckage that jerk created is still unravelling. Going to have to look at that footage, stay away from the computers, and concentrate on the drugs for now.

I get out the memory cards and the list Bob's people had put together. Looking at Bob's list, I realize I have not even glanced at it. I look and see everything is dated, listed like my memory cards. The others by Frank, and a few other sources, are also listed. I see there are a bunch of memory cards with Mike on them, dated before Louisa was murdered.

I turn my computer on and slip in the first one. Mike is there getting high, acting very strangely, running around the room and talking aloud. He thinks somebody is in the room with him, but nobody is there. He starts throwing punches at empty air. He opens the door and tells them to leave. I knew Mike had been doing a lot of drugs, but to act that way he had to have been doing more than I suspected.

I fast forward and see nothing I think is important. I

start another card. While the player is booting up I check the names on the other cards. One says, «Mike & unknown person.» I take out the other card and put this one in. When it finally comes up on the screen, Mike is on the phone. He's in a rundown, filthy room. He hangs up the phone, sits at a table, and starts snorting something that is probably cocaine.

Oh no, not more psychotic shit. The drugs are starting to take hold. He starts looking around. It looks like he is looking at something. The doorbell rings. Mike jumps up and grabs a very large knife. He lunges at the figure in the open doorway. He stumbles and sticks the knife in the doorframe. The guy in the doorway is incredibly fast. He swings with a left. Mike cracks his head on the doorframe. It might be the drugs he is doing, but Mike does not go down. Up until now, I had been concentrating on Mike and his actions. Suddenly it dawns on me; the guy in the door is my brother, Mark.

«What the fuck?» I yell to no one, totally surprised.

Mark comes in, kicks the door shut, and says, «I've wanted to do this ever since I met you.» Mike is shaking his head trying to focus. Mark punches Mike, one each to the head, stomach, chin and a knee to the groin. Mike goes down.

Mark is so fast it's hard to believe. The look on his face is pure joy; he is doing something he loves. I have never seen this side of my brother. What I remember the most about him was he was always high. It's been a lot of years since I have seen him. He looks fit and muscular, many hours in the gym I think. He walks over to Mike and gives him a kick.

«Weak, fucking pansy,» he says, kicking him out of the way. «Weak, fucking pansy»—where have I heard that lately? I have not heard «pansy» for years, but I know I've heard it lately. Part of a recovering addict's problem is the loss of short-term memory. Sometimes, when you hear or see something, it does not register. You forget for a while, but sometimes it sinks in after a few days or maybe a week. I have learned not to force it to come. If I do, it seems to take longer.

Mark is looking around the room, a filthy little place. He throws a mirror with drugs on it against the wall, white powder everywhere. He goes to the sink, fills a pot with cold water, and throws it on Mike. Mike wakes up and looks around as if he doesn't know where he is.

«I told you no fucking drugs today, man. We got some business to do. You fuck it up, you're dead,» Mark warns Mike.

The Mark I see on the computer screen is not at all like my brother, a stranger, a very hard, cold person.

«Go get cleaned up,» he yells at Mike. Mark looks as if he has been clean and sober for quite awhile. Mike is obviously afraid of him and heads to the shower. Mike's eyes are almost closed now, the swelling covering most of his face.

«Soak your face in cold water until the swelling goes down. You can't do this if you can't see.» I remember the movie Rocky a long time ago, his eyes so swollen he could not see. That's what Mike looks like now.

«I'll be back in a while. You be ready, or you'll be sorry. Me and Louise are getting back together, maybe, and I have to go see her.» He goes out the door.

I recall seeing Mike all beat up a few times before, years ago and about two months before Louisa's murder. Both eyes were black, two of his front teeth missing.

Mike looks around for his drugs. He is in a lot of pain. He sees the mirror, goes over to it on the ground. There is a little pile of blow on the floor. He gets a playing card and scrapes it up, rubs it on his gums, snorts the rest, dirt and all.

About ten minutes later Mark walks back in.

«You better pull this off. Nobody rips me off and gets away with it. I'm giving you this one chance. You fuck it up, you won't be on the planet any more. Is this how you operate? Do a deal with someone, spend his money, and steal his dope? Do a deal with another person and give his money to the first guy you ripped off?

«You got caught this time. Lucky for you I'm so forgiving. I should have listened to Chris. He said you were a loser and a rip off.»

«I'm sorry. I just got into it and could not stop. I always make it up,» Mike whines.

«You're lucky I need this deal; otherwise what you got earlier will just be the beginning,» Mark warns.

«What time is it? I need a couple of lines. I can't think straight it hurts so much,» Mike says.

«Too bad—suffer. You don't have to think. Maybe you'll learn a lesson from this. Time to go.» They walk out the door.

What has happened to Mark? It's good that he is fit as he is. Obviously, he has stopped using drugs, but now he's so vicious and violent. I can see he really liked hurting Mike. What has changed him so much? I know his lifestyle is very different from mine. He gets off on the excitement of it all.

I remember the last time I saw him we were at his place, catching up a bit. There was a woman who was nodding off in a chair in the corner. She woke up, reached under her cushion, and pulled out a loaded gun. She pointed it all around the room pretending to shoot everybody. She looked at the clock and said, «Time to go.» She put the gun in her purse, and the other three people got up.

Mark said to me, «Okay, Chris, I gotta get going. Good

to see you. Come by again sometime, and we'll catch up some more.»

I never did go back. At school, Mark was always a chubby kid, getting picked on all the time. Looking at him now, you would have to be crazy or have a death wish to go after him.

There does not seem to be any more on the video card. I look through the pile for others with the same date. One says, «Mike and Bill and unknown person,» with the same date. I stick it in. I figure the video cards are copies and have been edited for content, the dead time erased. I know the cops cannot have tampered with the originals, or they would be no good for evidence.

Think I will copy them for myself. I have a few blanks, so I put the first one back in and copy it. It's less than a quarter full. I put the other video in and copy it also, and do the same with all the rest.

At least I don't have to worry about the law. My ignorance of the rules does not matter to me. My law is turning out to be an eye for an eye. Knowing I am starting to feel very violent about revenge, I can see how Mark might be feeling the same way. We were both druggies. We do not like to be pushed around and react quickly when the need arises. The only difference I can see is that I do not enjoy it. Actually, to be honest, I did not enjoy the violence before; but lately I am enjoying it more and more. That's something I want to put an end to. I want justice, not another drug.

Mark said he and Louise were getting back together, something I know from experience does not work. Louise told me they had broken up long ago. I will have to talk with Louise to see exactly when they broke up.

I phone Margaret. Just to hear her voice sends shivers up

and down my back. «Can you do me a favour,» I ask her.

«Sure,» she says.

«Could you get Amy to ask Julie when she and Mark broke up, before or after Louisa was killed?»

«I already know,» she says. «They were together two or so months before, but she said some woman kept calling, and she could not take it. She moved out again but continued to see him for a couple of weeks before calling it quits for good. When you spend that many years together, you owe it to yourself to see if it really is over,» Margaret says.

«Do you know if she has seen him since?» I ask her.

«No, she said it was as if he had fallen off the face of the earth. She has not heard of him for a few years or so. I know all this because we were sitting here talking about this very thing a day or two ago. We want very much to help you, Chris,» Margaret tells me.

«Okay, thanks. That clears things up a bit, gets me thinking about a few things.

«How would you like it if I take you out for a nice, romantic dinner, go back to your place for a perfect ending to the night?» I ask her.

«Oh yes, I would like that very much.»

«Can I ask another favour? I need some more memory cards. Can you pick me up three or four?»

«I'll go to the store in a few minutes. See you at about 7:30?» she asks.

«Okay, see you at your place 7:30.» I hang up and go back to the computer.

Chapter 22

I start the second card. Mike is standing in the open doorway, Mark standing behind him.

Bill says, «Come in. You must be Mark.»

«Maybe,» says Mark walking in the door, Mike following him. Mike is carrying a bag.

«What the fuck happened to you, Mike?» Bill asks

«I got beat up,» he says. What do you think?»

«Looks painful, and you're still bleeding. Go wash up. I don't want your blood all over the place. Leave the bag here, not that I don't trust you,» Bill says.

«Don't worry about him for now. I just tuned him up for taking some. Let's go outside. We need to talk, away from Mike,» Mark suggests. They go outside. So Mark knew Mike, now Bill. How deep was his connection to all this? I wonder what Mark looks like today, after all these years. Is he still taking care of himself? Louisa was still alive when this video was taken. Mike comes back in the room, sees nobody there, and starts searching the place. He opens a drawer and smiles. He takes some money and what looks like a fold of coke. He goes back into the bathroom a few minutes before Mark and Bill come back.

«Come on, Mike. Let's go,» Mark yells. Mike comes out of the bathroom. It does not look like he is in pain anymore. They leave, and the bag stays there. So Mark and Bill met just before Louisa was killed. Is there a connection? I look at another card. It says, «Mike, Bill, Art, and Mark.» This one is dated a few days after the other one. I stick it in the computer. Mike is at the door, Mark beside him.

Bill is saying, «Come on in.» He looks at Mike and hits him in the face, taking him by surprise.

Mike, almost screaming, asks, «What the fuck was that for?»

«The two hundred dollars and the gram of coke you stole from me when you were here last time. Get the fuck out of here, and don't come again until you pay me back.» He goes to hit him again, but Mike runs out the door before he can.

«Fucking weak pansy,» Mark says.

«Yeah,» replies Bill.

«The money and coke in the drawer were for Mike anyway. He stole what was his,» Bill chuckles. «Except he shorted himself five hundred dollars.» There it is again, «Fucking weak pansy.» I still do not remember where I've heard it. Sitting on the couch, Art is there. Bill introduces Art as his partner to Mark. They don't shake hands. Bill hands Mark an Adidas bag. Mark looks inside.

«Do I have to count it?» he asks.

«No, it's all there.»

«You want to do this again?» Mark asks.

«Yes, but I don't know exactly when. One week or two,» Bill tells him.

«Okay. You know how to reach me?»

So, now he's met Art, and they are all in business together. Mark was smart having Mike give the bag to Bill, coming back a couple of days later for the money. Who's to say what transpired? I need to talk with Frank about the videos.

I call him up and ask, «What about the first videos of

Mike and the ones with Mark in them? How come there was no follow up on them?»

«That was when we were first watching Mike. At first all we saw were videos of him getting high. We followed him and saw who he was dealing with. We finally got a camera into Bill's apartment, but he moved abruptly, before we could get the video. We did not know what was recorded. By the time we got to see it, Bill had disappeared; and we did not know anything about Mark at all. When we finally found Bill again, Mark was nowhere to be seen.»

«So you did not know that Mark is my brother?» I ask.

«What? He's your brother?»

«Yeah, you mean you still don't know he is my brother?»

«We never saw him again and did not look for him at all,» Frank explains.

«I wonder what he's been doing all these years, and where he is now,» I wonder out loud.

«Maybe Louise can tell us, or maybe she can find him,» Frank suggests.

«Yeah, maybe. I'm having dinner with Margaret tonight. I will get her to ask Louise.» After I hang up, I can't help but think of Mark. He seems to have more drug connections than he used to. High quality coke and heroin. From what I remember, Mark was using way too much to be trusted by any but the smallest dealers. They would not have trusted him enough to front him then. To gain these connections he would have to be drug free for quite a while. Since I have not seen him in years, that is very possible. Waiting for 7:30 is getting harder to do. I want to see Margaret so badly. The phone rings, and it's her.

«Frank called a few minutes ago and asked me to find

out more about Mark from Louise. I'll let you talk to her,»
Margaret says.

Louise comes on the line. «Hi Chris, how are you?»

«Okay and you?»

«Good. Margaret says you want to know about Mark?»

«Yes, it's important.»

«Okay. Mark got a job on the tugboats. He continued
to use a bit but slowly weaned himself off. When he was
offered a job on the international tugs, he stopped using
entirely. We were still living together, but he was gone three
weeks to a month at a time. It was getting harder and harder
to stay together. I found out he was seeing a woman named
Julie, and I told him to fuck off.

«That was about four months before Louisa was killed,»
she explains. «He said he was taking time off work so we
could patch things up. He told Julie we were going to get back
together, and he could not see her. I moved back in for two
months, but he started seeing Julie again. I moved out. He kept
calling me saying if we didn't get back together again, he was
going to start using again. I heard a voice in the background
say something about him being a 'pansy.' He hung up, and
that was the last time I heard from him. Does that help?»

«More than you can imagine,» I assure her. So Julie was
with Mark. Thanks to Louise I remember where I'd heard,
«Weak, fucking pansy.» When I was at work Julie had said,
«weak, fucking pansy» about her brother and her dad. When
I worked there previously, Mark had come by a few times.

Was he there to see me, or Julie? She had been working
in the office answering phones, typing and such. It's amazing
the things you can learn just from talking to people. I am
normally not good at talking with people, especially small
talk. With cocaine you isolate because of the paranoia. You

do not trust anyone. All social skills are lost. In fact most skills are. The longer you use, the fewer skills you have. I have to work on that.

When I go to work tomorrow, if Julie is there, I will ask her about Mark. If she won't talk to me, I'll follow her home. Guess I'll have to borrow Margaret's car.

Chapter 23

If what I am beginning to think is what happened, I will not have any proof. I am going to have to set the stage. It is going to get very dangerous, so I need to arrange for the girls' safety. I have already lost one person whom I thought I could not live without. I'll be fucked if I am going to lose another. I call Frank and ask him to meet us at the restaurant at 9:00 p.m. I need some time to be alone with Margaret.

After an enjoyable dinner, we sit and talk a bit. I tell her, «Frank is meeting us here soon. There is something I am going to ask you to do, and I want no argument. Oh, here is Frank now, so hold on a sec, and I'll fill you both in.»

«Hi guys,» Frank smiles. «What's up, Chris?»

«I talked with Louise, and I think either Mark or Julie hired Bill and Art to kill Louise, not Louisa. I have no proof, but I know if I make them paranoid about things, the guilty party will try to kill me outright, or will hire somebody to do it. I have a feeling they don't even know Louise is still alive,» I explain.

«Margaret, remember Bill and Art talking. One of them said, 'We can't tell Gord we killed the wrong bitch.' They will come after either me or Louise.» Frank and Margaret are looking at me with disbelief. They both start to talk at once.

«Hey man, I can't let you do this. What you say makes so much sense, but what you suggest is too dangerous,»

Frank says, butting in forcibly.

«Yeah,» Margaret adds.

«Well, you don't have a say in this. All I need you to do, Frank, is hide the girls and protect them. No way will I allow them to be hurt.» They both look at me for a while and obviously realize I am going to do this no matter what they say or do. «Can I count on you to look out for the women, Frank?» I ask.

«You know you can, Chris. What are you going to do?»

«I will have to find Mark and talk with him, and Julie— ask if they've seen Louise. If I'm right, one or both will tell me she is dead. I'll know then what I believe is right.»

«Margaret, I was going to ask you to come home with me tonight, but I need you to go talk with Amy and Louise. Pack some stuff and let Frank take you somewhere safe. And Margaret, you have to stay put. Please don't try to come and help. This is going to take a while. Frank, no phone calls for the girls, okay,» I say, clearly setting the rules.

«I will phone the cops after I talk with Mark and Julie, so I won't be in danger. Okay?» I get up, give them both hugs, pay the bill, and leave. I do not intend to phone the police. I have waited far too long for this revenge. After leaving the restaurant, I go to Len's apartment. With or without his permission I am going to use it. It will be even better if he is already there, locked in his own chains, gagged, and helpless. I have big plans for him, also. There are some heavy bars in the room with places to attach chains.

Eyebolts are set in the ceiling. I place a bar with some weights on the ends and check the weight. It is very heavy. If somebody were hit with this, they would be out of action for a long time, maybe even dead. I arrange the pulley system so I can pull the bar to the ceiling. I attach one end to the doorknob. If the door opens, the bar will come crashing down and hit the person coming in the door. I try it a couple of times. The first time one side hits first. I adjust the chains until both ends of the bar hit the wall at the same time. The noise the bar makes when it hits is loud. I pull the bar up, go out the door, and let the chain go. With the door open you can barely hear the bar hit, just a slight vibration.

Perfect! Len must have spent a lot of money fixing this room up. That should take care of one of them, now to figure a way to stop the other. I'm counting on at least two people coming, maybe three. While I'm strong, fast, and know how to throw a punch, I don't want to take any chances. I don't have a gun and don't want to get one. I decided on a baseball bat. I need to knock them out and tie them up very quickly. I plan to let them get into the apartment with ease and will wait in one of the bedrooms.

I find some twine and run it to the second bedroom with one end tied to a bottle. The other end is tied to the top of the front door. When the door opens, the bottle will fall, warning me. Next, I place a radio in the bondage room. I cannot find a long extension cord, so I make a mental note to get one. I also need a drill so I can thread the extension cord though the wall. When I hear the bottle drop, I will wait a short time and then plug the radio in. Hearing the radio come on, they will hopefully think I am in that room.

For some reason my plan makes sense. I know Julie is an extremely jealous person. Mark telling her he was getting back with Louise is something she could not stand. With his continued interest, it probably made it worse. I have a feeling Mark and Julie think Louise is dead. They both disappeared shortly after Louisa's death. I also think Mark was behind the heroin and coke smuggling. He likely made connections on his tugboat trips. I have to talk with him to know for sure, but I'm positive I am right. There are simply too many people and things coming together in one place to be just coincidence, including Julie showing up right after the shipment was taken by the police. I have to talk with Mark, if he will talk with me. Tomorrow I will get the extension cord and drill. All I need to do now is let Mark and Julie know where I'm going to be. I have to find them.

Chapter 24

My mind keeps coming back to that phrase, «weak, fucking pansy.» I remember hearing Julie say it. I also remember hearing Margaret say it the day we overheard Bill and Art at the treatment centre. Also, Margaret lied about being there because of drugs, yet Frank said it was because of her worrying about me. I'm freaking out now! Am I just getting paranoid again, or is there something to it? God I hope not. I'm thinking the druggie never gets the girl. Is that what it is, my own self-worth getting in the way? Enough of that, one way or another I will find out.

I decide to sleep in Art's room, the one farthest from the front door. I am too tired to walk home. Besides, the hardware store is just around the corner. I put the bottle where it will make a noise if it falls. Just in case, I set up the bar, taking the weights off. I leave the light on in the bondage room. I go to Art's room, lie down, and start to fall asleep.

I wake up with a start. What's that noise? I look around. The bottle has fallen to the floor. I get up and listen at the door, hear a loud grunt, and I run into the room. Len is on the floor doubled over, gagging and cannot breath. The wind is knocked out of him. I pump on his stomach and pound on his back until he is breathing okay. I don't want him dying on me just yet. I drag him over to the bondage rack, chain him up, gag, and blindfold him. It's a good thing I took the weights off, or he would probably be dead. It worked perfectly, sort of filled me with a bit of pride.

Funny how things work out. Len is exactly where I want him, and he walked right into it. Nobody will ever know I am involved. Just like I want and need it to be. It's time for me to find out if the computer's password has been bypassed, or whatever it is they do. I double check Len's bindings, cuff his hands above his head, and immobilize his legs. He starts to wake up.

When he is fully aware, I tell him, «I want you to hang here and think about your past, think really hard about all the things you have done. You are about to experience some of them yourself. I just hope you live long enough to suffer a fraction of what you have caused others. I'm going to leave you now. Think about these things and grow just a little bit frightened.»

I go home to get my laptop and videos of Len. I get to my apartment, find the videos and laptop, and phone my friend about the computers. «I'll call my friend and call you back,» he says.

«Good, I'll be waiting.»

He calls back in about twenty minutes. «Yes, they're open. Come by in about an hour and they'll be here.»

«Great, do you think he looked at what's in it?»

«He says not, but you never know. See you soon.»

He is not at his store when I arrive. Turns out he's gone on an installation and will be gone for hours. My computer was there, a paper taped to it. On the paper are a password and a bill for two hundred dollars. I pay the cashier, pick up a few more cameras, and return to Len's apartment. I watch some of the videos while hooking up Bruce's computer to Len's monitor, keyboard, mouse, and speakers. I go into the kitchen waiting for it to boot up. Good, he has coffee, sugar, and milk.

After pouring a coffee I go back to the videos. These are videos taken outside his building. Not much happening except for a lot of young girls coming and going. I watch closely to see if they look different coming out of the apartment. A lot of them are crying and not walking very well. All the girls are pretty, and they all look stoned. One girl reminded me of Margaret, but oh so young. She looks so dejected. Bruce's computer is finally ready, so I enter the password. It's Bruce's birthday. I open documents and see files with Art, Len, and Bruce, to name a few.

Right now I want to look at Len's file. I open it, and there are photographs, still shots, and videos. I click on one video. Len is in his room dressed in leather with a whip in his hand. A girl is dangling from chains, her back covered in welts. There is no blood. The girl is screaming in agony.

Len says, «Who are you, and what are you?»

«Fuck off,» she screams at him. He continues to whip her.

«Who are you, and what are you?» he asks her again.

«Fuck off,» she repeats in a whisper, tears flowing freely from her eyes.

He picks up a cattle prod and delivers an electric shock to her groin. She is so weak by now she can barely scream.

Once again he asks, «Who are you, and what are you?»

She is trying to talk, but it comes out a croak, not recognizable as words. Len gets a water bottle and squirts it in her mouth.

He asks again, «Who are you, and what are you?»

«I am your slave, and I am whatever you want me to be,» she says, obviously defeated.

«Good,» says Len, letting her down. «Now, suck it bitch,» he demands. «On your knees.» She crawls over to him and does as instructed. Sickened by this, I quickly copy it to a flash drive and put it into my laptop. I walk into the room where Len is still dangling and put it in front of him.

«I brought you some home movies so you won't get bored,» I seethe, and turn it on. He is making noises as if he wants to say something, but it is all garbled. I get the whip and the cattle prod. The first stroke takes him completely by surprise.

«This is going to be your life, at least what life you have left. I'm going to leave you for a while, look around the apartment. We'll have a little talk when I get back, okay?» I see tears in his eyes, and he won't look at me. «See, this is how that girl felt when you had control of her. Get used to it, asshole.»

All the exercise and anger has made me hungry. I go to the kitchen and look in cupboards and drawers. Len seems to like to eat well. There are little piles of money and drugs in every drawer. I decide I have to clean it up. I gather up the drugs, bag them to give to Frank. I keep some heroin and a needle. Len is going to become a junkie.

I count the money, a little over two thousand dollars in the kitchen alone. I cook a steak, baked potato, and creamed corn. Len has very good taste in coffee. I have three cups. I figure Len is hungry, but he is also a little fat. I'll let him live on that for a while.

Of course, I have been worrying about infection. I am not very good with the whip, and he has cuts everywhere. I find an empty three-litre milk container, put half a box of salt in, and add some boiling water so all the salt will dissolve. Salt is very good for killing germs, has some very good healing properties. I go back to see him, tune him up a bit more. Oh man, look at that. I made more cuts.

«Hey, Len, I think you are going to be here for a while, and I am worried about infection, so I brought in a big container of salt water. It will take care of that.» I hear his screams from behind the gag. «Aww, Len, quit screaming and crying. It had to be done, for your own good,» I tell him. «See you in a while. You just hang in there. Be good.»

I am having too much fun. I go into the other room, pour another coffee, and boot up the laptop. Waiting, I start thinking about Mark again. Did he want to get rid of Louise because she wanted to break up? I do not want to think so, but is that because he is my brother and I want him to be better than that? I hope he has nothing to do with it. What I saw of him on the computer before impressed me. What can I say against his cruelty? Is what I am doing to Len the same?

«Sometimes one needs a bit of violence in his life, not only for the excitement, but also to protect people,» I justify out loud to no one. «Getting a little violent with someone can help him. Keep the other person in line so that person does not hurt himself. There are so many reasons for it. Who is right and who is wrong?»

Anybody can justify it to himself, make it okay. Governments do it all the time—for «their own» protection is their favourite lie.

What do I know about Julie except she is mean, spoiled, jealous, with no personality to speak of, and oh yeah, a real bitch? She is extremely good looking, which she uses to get what she wants. All in all, a very unpleasant creature. I think she is more than capable of hiring somebody to kill a person. Hell, I even think she could do the killing herself.

I see the computer is up and running, so I open Len's files, preparing for some horrible things. This time there are two girls in the room, one chained like the first. The other one is kneeling at her feet. Art is in this video. I look more closely. The girls are twins. Man, I can't take this, have to watch it later. I have to concentrate on finding Mark and learning about the others. I get up and check the rest of the apartment. I go into Len's bedroom, check all the drawers. In the top there is a small bundle of bills, next to the money, some drugs, which I think is heroin. Hey, I did not even think of that, drugs. I'm going to have to be careful around it.

I call Frank and tell him about the drugs I've found and want to get rid of them before I yield to temptation. I tell him to meet me at the park across from my apartment. I get the drugs, look in on Len, and pick up the whip; it was a complete surprise. Man, this is getting serious, the hate I feel for this man!

I notice there is something funny about him; he looks all white. I look closer and realize it's the salt. Oh, good, something is finally going right. I won't have to douse him again, just hose him down.

I meet Frank and give him the drugs, immediately feeling better. «Thanks, I wanted to get that off my hands.»

«Where did you get it?»

«I was at work, looking for Julie. I remembered the apartment upstairs and found it in there,» I tell him.

«Okay.»

«Did you get an idea about how to find Mark?» Frank asks me.

«No, not really. I will have to wait until my boss gets to work and talk to him,» I say.

«How's Margaret? Are she and the other girls in a safe place?» I ask Frank.

«Yeah. They are at Bob's, with a couple of uniforms there all the time. They're safe,» he says.

«Okay. That's a load off my mind. Tell her I love her and am thinking about her. Tell her not to worry. I'm going to work and see if Randy's dad is there. See you later.» I walk the short distance to work.

Someone is in the office. Maybe he's there. I go in; Julie is working on the computers. I see she is about to print something off. She looks at me and says, «Oh shit. What do you want?»

«I'm looking for my brother, Mark,» I tell her.

«Why would he want to talk with a weak pansy like you?» she asks.

I've never hit a woman in anger before, but my feelings for this woman almost make me. I move toward her with my hand upraised, but I can't hit her. I want her mad at me, and this is the perfect opportunity. Why can't I hit her? «Listen, bitch, I've heard enough out of your fucking mouth. Either you tell me where he is, or I'll make you very sorry.»

«I'm right behind you, Chris,» a voice says from behind me. «I know she can be horrible, but you can let her alone now.» I turn around. Mark is standing there looking tanned and very fit. I let go of Julie's hair and move towards the wall. I don't want to be in the middle of the room if something happens. Julie lunges at me, but Mark calls out, «Not now, Julie, maybe later.»

«Well, Chris, it's been a long time. I see you are pretty fit. Not doing drugs anymore?»

«No, clean for about six or seven months now,» I tell him.

«Last time I saw you was at Louisa's funeral. You were so high you didn't even know I was there,» he says.

«Yeah, I was in a bad way. Did not care about anything,» I answer, looking him in the eye.

«Weak fuck,» Julie starts to say, but before she can finish Mark says: «Shut up bitch. This is my brother. Don't talk.»

«Yes, sir!» Julie says.

The change that comes over her is immediate. She kneels down, her eyes resting on the floor. Mark says, «Stay there.»

«Yes, sir,» Julie replies.

«I see questions in your eyes,» Mark says to me. «Come upstairs, and we'll talk.» He looks at Julie. «Don't move. Don't even think.»

«Yes, sir,» she says, without looking at him.

The door to the upstairs apartment is open, and we go up. He goes into the kitchen and grabs me a Pepsi. «You still drink these?»

«Yup, that and lots of coffee.»

«Well, I guess you want to know what that was all about downstairs,» he asks.

«Very much so,» I say, with surprise in my voice.

«Well, it all started when we were both using. I was trying to stop and having a little success. I even got a job on the tugboats, working the harbour for twelve hours a day. We were both trying to quit the dope. When I was at work, she would sneak some. I could tell when I got home. It was hard for me to stay straight while she was getting high. When I was home, it was worse. I finally got stoned for one day. I almost lost my job. I got angry, turned her over my knee, and spanked the living shit out of her. It turns out she liked it very much. Her dad and Randy were 'weak pansies,' she said. Her mom would order them around, hit them both, and treated them like dirt. She was not used to a strong man. She liked the spanking and to be told what to do.»

Mark sees I want to talk and says, «Let me finish. I have not told this to anybody before, and if you interrupt, I won't be able to tell it right. Okay?» I nod.

«Anyway, I did not especially like hitting a woman, but she said she loved it, that it made the sex wonderful.

Almost like 'make-up' sex. Anyway, we started reading about BDSM—you know—bondage, discipline, sadism, and masochism. We started to practise it, slowly at first, and we got into it more and more.

«Julie became so submissive to me I could not stop. She would do anything I wanted. I like a lot of it, but not all the time. Julie wants it all the time. I need to feel normal; to me it is just exciting sex, for her a lifestyle. She also hates weak men, calls them, 'weak, fucking pansies.'

«That was the phrase her mother used when she hit her dad and brother. I did not know that when I was off working Julie was practising bondage and other things with girls. She was the dominant one. She kept that a secret from me for years. Actually, I just found that out when we arrived back here. A very good-looking woman came to visit, and she was very submissive to Julie. Julie wanted to have a threesome, so we did. Julie told me the woman and her went way back, a very special relationship. They went to school together.

«Anyway, that's the story of Julie, and why she is still downstairs. I find the submissiveness very helpful at times. Does that answer all your questions?» he asks. I nod yes.

«Man, it's good to see you after all these years. I know the things I was into kept you away, but that's in the past. I'm in business now. Yes, the drug business, but no violence,» Mark says. «I had different jobs on the tugs, finally on boats going to Mexico, then South America. I started smuggling pot, but that was too bulky and smelly. Anyway, I eventually got into the coke and heroin business. I was going to bring you into it, but you were so fucked up over Louisa you would have been useless. Anyway, I was living in Brazil.

«Julie got the idea of bringing her brother, Randy, into the picture. The result is my last shipment and part of the one before has now been taken by the police. Anyway, I stayed in Brazil while Julie came up every month to keep an eye on things. I think she has been involved in other things but has not said a word, one of the only things she keeps from me. She seems to have lots of money, and none of the drug money is ever missing.»

Sensing that he has stopped talking, I break in, «When did you start seeing Julie?»

«I met her when you were working here before. We hit it off right away.»

«You were with Louise still?»

«Yeah, off and on. As I said, I got a job on the tugs and was there a few years. When we finally broke up, I got on the international runs. Julie's jealous nature showed its ugly head for the first time then. When Louise died, that's when I decided to move to Brazil. My business was starting to take off.» I butt in before he can continue.

«You mean when Louisa died. Louise is still a friend of mine, and I saw her not too long ago, a day or two at most.»

«What do you mean—not dead?» he says, his facing going white. «I saw her body. Her face was all smashed in, but I know it was her. Same hair, same ears, it was her. I know it was.» He shakes his head in disbelief and says, «You sure?»

«Very,» I say «I also think Julie knows she is still alive. Whose idea was it to move to Brazil—Julie's, right?» I ask.

«Yes, it was. Julie, get up here you stupid little whore, right now!» he yells. She immediately runs upstairs.

«What's this? Louise is still alive?» he says to her. «Who was the girl I saw in the morgue?» She looks startled and then looks at me with hate in her eyes.

«What?» she says, playing the dumb bitch. We can both

tell by the guilt written all over her face she knows.

I've learned what I had set out to—time to go. I have to change my plan. Margaret knows too much of it. I cannot use Len's apartment for the trap. I will have to use my apartment.

«Looks like your hands are full here. Why don't we get together in a day or two—when things have cooled down a bit between the two of you?» I give Mark my address and phone number. Julie glares at me. She hears the laughter in my voice. It is not a funny situation at all, but she knows I am laughing at her. She knows I hate her guts. She gives me an «if looks could kill, you'd be dead» kind of look. I've had a few of those recently.

I have many questions for Mark; however, the one on my mind is, who was the good-looking woman Julie had the special relationship with? I already know the answer. I have known for a while now—Margaret. She is very submissive, always doing what I want, hardly ever on her own volition. Also, the phrase Margaret has used, «weak, fucking pansy.» I know by that comment alone she knows Julie. Why is this so complicated? All I wanted was to see some dealers in jail and the ones who killed Louisa dead. I hate everything, everyone involved in this stinking mess, but I cannot stop now. People have to pay, an eye for an eye.

On the way out I turn the camera back on.

Chapter 25

My thoughts go back to the «other woman» in the threesome. I know it's Margaret. I don't want her anywhere near me when this next scenario unfolds. I can only accommodate so many people at a time at Len's, and Julie will be a nice companion for him. Margaret knows about the secret door into the apartment. I am positive that's the way the intruders will come in. If that is how they will come in for the attack on me, it will be final proof of Margaret's involvement.

I phone Bob, suggesting Margaret go to a meeting, so she has an opportunity to phone Julie.

«Are the girls okay? I think Margaret should probably go to a meeting. She must be stressed beyond belief.»

«Actually, she did want to go to one, but I told her no. But I guess you're right. We don't want her relapsing.»

«Good, send an officer with her but have him wait outside. It is supposed to be addicts only. If a cop walks in, the addicts won't feel safe again.»

«You got it. I know how meetings work,» he tells me.

«I want a cop there so she goes back to your place. She might try to come and help me. I cannot have that. I am really worried about her safety.»

«Sure,» he confirms.

«I'll tell her she can go now if she wants to. Take care,

and keep up the good work.»

I've done what I can—given Margaret a chance to contact Julie yet also made sure she will not be at the apartment. I need time to decide on Margaret's punishment. After all, it must fit the crime, and when it comes, be swift and sure. It will be very hard to fall in love again. It's too painful. Trust has always been hard for me. Now it will be even harder.

I know by Julie's reaction she has not talked with Margaret recently. The look she gave me was one of distaste, not a frightened, hateful one. Why I am taking this all so calmly? I love Margaret, so why no tears? One of the things a drug addict loses is the ability to trust, to truly let go and allow someone into your heart. You become hardened to normal emotions. You might fall in love, but not fully and completely. There's always a part of you that holds back, the part where you hurt them, the part where they desert you. There are so many ways to get wounded and to wound somebody else. I feel the beginnings of tears, but I know they won't come.

Emotions you do not lose include sadness, compassion, and a desire to stop people from walking in your shoes. Many recovering addicts want to become counsellors, to help. I know I did. I have shed tears for other people seeing the hurt and turmoil they are in. I can cry for them but have not been able to for myself in a very long time. I started all this revenge stuff so I could die, but in the end it's my desire to help others that has kept me clean and made me strong.

I think of poor Amy. Margaret knew all along what was happening to her. Did she not want to look after her? Did she want her out of the way? Thinking of Amy and the pain she has felt makes me start to cry. I don't know when my tears for her turn into ones for myself. Tears are the way a person lets go. To shed a tear for a lost one is a natural thing. I have lost Margaret, but did I ever really have her? No!

I feel clearer in my head now, and I know when the time comes I can do what has to be done. In the past I have broken up with numerous women and felt emptiness. I do not feel any emptiness right now. She has betrayed not only me but also her family. She has to be taught a lesson. Betrayal is one of the ultimate sins in my opinion.

You put all of your love, trust, and loyalty in one person, and when that is taken away, you are left with emptiness, loneliness, and despair. Well, fuck that. She is the empty one, not Amy, Frank, or me. My trouble is I try to think of everything because a mistake may cost some innocent person dearly. I cannot have that on my conscience.

Sometimes, simple is the best way. I know that in my apartment there are only a few ways to get in—windows, front door, and the door to the adjoining room. They will think I am inside my room. I will be in the other one. When they come in, I will get them from behind. Maybe I'll put a board with some nails in it just inside both doorways and by the window. It will be awful hard not to cry out with a nail in the foot. I'll get it ready tomorrow if it's not too late.

I watch a lot of movies and get ideas from them. The dropping weight was from one movie, a comedy. The show's star wanted to keep his victims out. I want to let them in and keep them there, preferably unconscious and tied up. This is very real, and it's certainly not funny. Well, the look on their faces might be.

I decide to videotape the event to relive the moment, but also because it might be useful to clear my name. I want this revenge to be close and very personal. I want them to suffer for the rest of their lives. I go into the other apartment; it is almost empty except for a couch by the window. I go to my apartment, grab a whole bunch of blankets and pillows and arrange them behind the couch.

What can I use as a weapon? I don't have a baseball bat, but another movie comes to mind, one with Sean Penn. He gets two Pepsi's and puts them in a pillowcase. Lucky for me I have both. Maybe I should use Coke because «things go better with Coke.»

I decide to make it three cans, just in case I hit someone and the cans empty. Man, that's what I mean, over-thinking again. I put three cans into three different pillowcases. I put two inside my apartment near the doors. The other I tie to my wrist so if I fall asleep, I won't have to look for it. Another movie comes to mind, this one with Mel Gibson. A paranoid nutcase in this movie, Gibson's character puts a bottle on the doorknob and when somebody tries the door, it falls. I put one on each knob. There are hardwood floors in both apartments, so I will hear them when or if they fall.

I also grab a few Pepsi's for myself, a bag of chips, and my portable DVD player. I may as well be comfortable while I wait for my revenge.

CHAPTER 26

I open a pop, turn on the DVD player, and lie down to wait, hopefully, not for long. It would be comforting to have someone else here for back-up, but this has to be done for me and by me. If I fail, no one else will be hurt. I remember the last time I was lying behind a couch. It brings back very painful memories, lying there with Margaret hearing Art and Bill talking. Those same emotions come to the surface, but this time my rage is not so hot. I'm cooler—calm and collected.

I pity the poor fuck that comes through that door. I hope it comes down to a real life and death battle. I finish the last of my Pepsi. The movie is almost over when I hear the bottle dropping to the floor. I turn the DVD off thinking, Oh shit, now I'll miss the end of the movie. I grab the pillowcase and get ready to go into action. My heart is racing, arms trembling with tension as the anger fills my mind. The door opens, and one person walks through the door. Do I know who it is?

He kicks the bottle away, not caring about the noise. He looks around searching for something. He spots the connecting door, walks right up to it as if he knows it is there. Oh well, I knew Margaret was involved, so why this bitter disappointment? He has something in each hand, a knife in one and what looks like a cattle prod in the other. Who is it?

I know him; it's the guy that was in charge of the supply room at work. Since he's alone, I decide to take him in this apartment. Keep mine nice and neat. He has to use one of his hands to open the door. Which one is he going to put down? Oh good, the prod. He puts it in his back pocket.

«Oh shit,» he says. He forgot to turn it off and gave himself a shock. This is going to be too easy. Almost laughing aloud, I watch him dance around. Maybe this is more like that comedy than I thought. As he slowly gets over the shock, he moves toward the door. I walk up behind him, tap him on the shoulder.

«What the—» is all he has time to say before his lights go out. The blow to his head was very satisfying, but somehow not enough. The cans of Pepsi do leak, a mess all over the floor. I turn him over, check his pulse. Oh man, there's nothing there.

I give him CPR, or what I hope is CPR. I feel a few ribs crack. Fuck, what am I gonna do with him? I look more closely at him. God, I do know him. It's Julie and Randy's brother. I saw him only once before. Funny I did not recognize him before. Fuck, what am I gonna do now? I hear a moan. Oh, thank you, God. I use my belt to tie him up. Good thing I had the camera on. I will turn it and him over to the police.

I go into my apartment to think, shaking all over—shock, I guess. I grab some towels and start cleaning up the Pepsi. I stepped in it, and I got it in my apartment. Just then the phone rings. I pick it up, and it's Bob.

He says, «What are you doing? I have some news for you, not very good news.»

«Oh. I spilled some Pepsi and was just cleaning up.»

«Chris, Mark is dead. Julie's dad killed him. He says he

walked in on them. Julie was chained to a bench, and Mark was whipping her. He had heard her screaming when he was downstairs. He grabbed a chisel off a bench. The door was open; he made no noise coming in. He stuck the chisel in Mark's neck.»

«Oh. Okay,» Not really taking it all in. I tell him, «It should all be on video. I have a camera in there. I also have some news for you. Julie's other brother attacked me. He is unconscious on the floor in the next apartment. It is also on video.

«Fuck,» says Bob. «Not your night!»

«Send some cops over, will you? Where is Mark now? Up till now it was fun,» I tell him.

«Mark is still at the shop. Frank is there now,» Bob says

«Can I come over and see him before you take him away?» I ask.

«I guess, since it's you asking. But you should stay there while they pick up Julie's brother. I will get an officer to drive you here then take you to the station,» he informs me.

«Thanks. Are you at the shop?»

«No, but Frank is. See you there. I'm on my way now,» he says.

«Okay.» What a night. I knew Mark had to be punished, but he was my brother. It was a very big shock. What was I supposed to do? What was I supposed to feel?

This is probably the best way. After all, family is family. We are supposed to help each other, not hurt. I know now that Randy's dad is also involved, because on the second day I was back at work, Len said, «My boss told me to come here instead of him because of your falling out» —something like that.

Funny how you think of a person in a certain way. I

thought of him as Randy's dad, not by his name. I also knew it was Margaret who told him about the door. It was almost a relief, surprisingly very little pain. I guess this whole mess is making me expect less and less of people. If I thought all people were like this, what would I, or could I do? Well, I guess I have to go say good-bye to Mark, even though we barely had a chance to say hello.

Chapter 27

The police arrive to take Randy's brother away. He means so little to me I do not even ask his name. I had already copied what was on the memory card, just in case the cops take the card when they take him to the station. Another cop drives me to work, walks me in. Frank sees me and walks over.

«It's okay, officer. I'll look after him now. You can go back to your duties.»

«It's pretty messy,» he says to me as we walk up the stairs.

«Well, I have to say good-bye to him, see what happened.»

«Yeah, I understand.» Blood is everywhere. Mark is lying on his side. His hands tried to stop the flow of blood. Death took care of that for him. There is a weight lifters bench in the middle of the floor, O-rings bolted to the floor, handcuffs still attached, four pair.

«Julie was still chained on this when we got here, her dad off in the corner crying, Julie screaming at him, 'You fucking weak pansy, look what you did, look what you did,' over and over,» Frank tells me.

Her punishment has already started, I see. I take great pleasure in that. I hold Mark's hand a minute, saying good-bye. It makes me sad to see him this way, destroyed by drugs, a man without a conscience.

«Where is Julie, now?» I want to know. It's not over between us yet.

«At the hospital, I think.» Frank says.

«Did Bob tell you what happened to me tonight? Julie's brother tried to kill me. It was rather comical, but he gave me a scare. I thought I had killed him. I have it all on video. I need to go home and get some sleep. Can I come to the station tomorrow?

«Oh, one more thing, her dad is involved in the drugs coming in and out of this place.»

«How do you know that?» Frank asks me. I tell him what Len said about his boss.

«He wanted his son to stay home because of our confrontation. I have no real proof, but if you question him after this, I am sure he'll admit to it. After all he is a weak, fucking pansy.»

«Okay. I'll tell the detectives. They're good. If he is, they'll get it out of him.»

«Worth a shot,» I say.

«Okay. You can go. See you at the station tomorrow,» he orders me.

«Good night,» I say, walking off with a last look at Mark. I walk home, sadness mixed with elation, up and down. I'm an emotional roller coaster. I open my front door, turn around to close it, and see movement out of the corner of my eye. I move my head to the side and instantly feel a sharp pain in my shoulder. If I'd not moved, I would have been hit on the head. I move away in the other direction, taking the other person off guard. My arm is useless because of the blow, so I kick my attacker in the knee. I hear a snap and a shriek. It's a woman! I grab her club, a baseball bat, and knock her unconscious. It's Julie.

Excellent! I know exactly what am I going to do with her. When all of this comes out, the police are going to be looking for her. If she disappears, it will be assumed she is in hiding, not abducted. How am I going to get her to Len's? I look out the window, some cars parked out front. I look for her car keys, then find them in her coat pocket. There is an alarm on her key ring. I go to the window, press it, and see which car is hers.

She is semiconscious now, and I find if I guide her, she can walk, but with a limp. «Come on, Babe. It's me, Mark. We gotta get out of here,» I tell her. We get to the car, and I drive to Len's, only minutes away. I walk her up the stairs and take her in to where Len is. I gag her and chain her much like Len, putting a blindfold on her also. I have great plans for this bitch. I look at her. She is very beautiful.

«What should I do with you? I think I'll keep you here a few days until the police know of your involvement. Being a drug dealer, I know a lot of women in jail. When I visit them, they are going to be paying a lot of attention to you. They like to see a proud scheming bitch like you on your knees.

«When you get out, I'll be here waiting for you. I should whip you for trying to kill me, but you would enjoy that. Maybe I'll become your new master. Unlike Mark, I will enjoy that very much. Just want you to know that you're mine now. Get used to it.»

I tell her this to get her thinking how her life has suddenly changed. That's a very hard reality for someone like her to take. I have plans for this woman; she has only just begun to suffer. I have so much to do and can only concentrate my efforts on one person at a time. Len is up first. I go over and check on him, see he's messed himself. Oh well, leave him for a while. Julie will love the smell.

I give Len some water to drink. I see the salt on him still and dump some more water on him. His screams are very soothing. «Sorry I have not been able to pay much attention to you, but I have been very busy. I promise to see you tomorrow.» I leave the room, locking it. I notice something on the floor, tracks for a sliding door, or something like it. I look around to see what it could be for. I walk over to the entertainment center. There are wheels on the front, and the back is on the track. I move it, and when I am finished, the door to the bondage room is completely hidden. A sliding bolt locks it in position. Looking at it compared to the rest of the room, it is the logical place for it to be.

Man, I really have to check this place out. What else is hidden here? Well, almost everybody is taken care of, except for Margaret. I phone Bob to see if she is still there. She is. «I'll be right there,» I tell him.

I'm at his door in about twenty minutes. I am very sick and tired of all this, and I want it, no I need it, to be over. I have no plan; but I think when Margaret sees me, she will start to freak out. If I see that, I'll confront her with what I know and see what she does. She is in the kitchen sitting at the table. A uniformed cop is standing really close to her. I get the feeling he is flirting with her. He goes red in the face when he sees me. He turns around and finds something very interesting to look at out the window. Bob is sitting at the table, cleaning his gun. He is almost finished, just putting the bullets back in.

«Does Margaret know what's been happening tonight?» I ask Bob.

«No, not yet,» he says.

«Well, Julie's brother has been arrested for trying to kill me. He came in through the apartment next door. Mark is dead, killed by Julie's dad. Julie is in the hospital with whip marks all over her. A camera I planted in the apartment above the shop captured Mark's murder. It's been there since I went back to work. The police have it now and are looking at it.»

As I'm talking I see Margaret go white, red, white, and then very red. Worried, scared, man it was almost hypnotic to see the play of emotions on her face, fascinating. She sits there not saying a word. The cop has turned around again, still standing next to her. Margaret looks at him; his gun is in his holster, a piece of leather holding it in place. So fast I can scarcely believe it, she grabs it and shoots me. I am hit in the shoulder.

I see she is going to fire again. I hear a shot, waiting to feel the impact of another bullet. I see a little red hole appear in her forehead. A spray of red, white, and gray appear on the cop's uniform. I look at Bob. He looks at me.

I look at my arm and say, «Oh no, a matching hole. She shot me in the other arm.» The pain hits me like a wave, and I pass out.

Chapter 28

I wake up in a hospital room, the same fucking room as it turns out. I'm not in as bad shape as last time, despite a bullet hole in my shoulder. Relatively healthy and fit this time, not near death because of drug abuse and blood loss. The medical attention I received was immediate and therefore loss of blood was minimal. I've been shot in almost the same place as before, only in the other arm.

The doctor tells me I can go home as soon as I get dressed. Since I need a smoke, I get dressed and leave right away. I am surprised at my lack of interest in what has happened, probably emotional overload. I am just happy to be out of that fucking hospital room. There is no one in my room when I dress and no one I know in the hospital lobby as I depart. Everybody must think I will be out of commission for a while. Perfect.

I need to go to Len's, see how they are doing. I'm not sure how much time has passed, but they must need water. When I get to the apartment building this time, I look for a way to enter the building with less chance of being observed. A bit of a disguise might be in order. There are a few things I need to get done. I want to search his apartment more closely, get his bankcard, empty his account. He won't need it anymore, anyway.

Maybe I can do some good with the money. I have a

favourite show on TV about a serial killer who kills pedophiles, rapists, and murderers. He kills them outright. I think they should be made to suffer. If people thought that might happen to them, they might think twice about harming others. I doubt it, though—the thrill they probably get outweighs the threat. I think by making them suffer would be the justice they deserve.

The underground parking seems the best way to come and go. I decide to keep the place in Len's name. As long as the condo fees are paid, taxes and stuff, who will know he's gone? I'm about his size. If I wear similar clothes, I don't think anybody will know, or care. I actually now feel very comfortable being here, my home away from home.

Once in the apartment I grab some water and a bit of food. I move the entertainment center and give Len and Julie water. I make them clean themselves one at a time. Back on his bench I tell Len he is going to have a bit of a reprieve. The sound of the whip as it flies through the air is very satisfying, almost as enjoyable as his muffled screams. «Sorry, Len. I lied!»

I go into the other room and turn the computer on to watch more of Len's videos. I open Len's files preparing for some horrible things. This time there are two girls in the room chained up, similar to the last video. One girl is chained and dangling, the other one kneeling at her feet. Art is in this video. I look more closely. The girls are twins.

Art says to Len, «I'm going to enjoy this training. Not many times you get to work on twins.»

«Me, too, the buyer has very specific instructions, and the thought of them turns me on.»

What's this—a buyer? I had always figured they were simply forcing these girls into prostitution, making them heroin addicts so they would have to work the streets. Is there more to the perversions these people are up to? I'm so angry that I have to calm down. Gotta get outta here, get calm. I get up and decide to check on Len.

«I've just discovered something that turns my stomach, so much that if I don't leave now, I will end up killing you. I have much bigger plans for you than that.» I check his bonds, pull the chains tighter, making his arms stretch a little more. I go out the door. I don't even glance at Julie. I wander around not knowing where or even how long I walk. How do I deal with this bullshit? I'm a drug addict, not some heroic son of a bitch out to right all the wrongs in the world. I know this won't be the end of it. I have to do something, and it will have to be sooner not later. I'm calmer now, more focused. I go back to the apartment.

The pain in my shoulder is killing me. I look in his medicine cabinet and find some Tylenol 3's. I take three, have a coffee, and wait for the pain to fade. I don't really want the drugs. I hurt too much. After a while the pain is bearable. I go and check the rest of the apartment. Checking all the drawers in his bedroom, in the top one I find a small bundle of bills.

Hey, why didn't I think of that? He must have more money. I wonder if there is a safe. A prick like him is bound to have one, his trust in people long gone. I look behind pictures, under rugs. Eventually I find it in the closet. A combination lock, I wonder how long it will take to get the combination from Len. I get a pen and paper, go to Len.

Undoing one hand I put the pen in it and tell him, «Write the combination.» He tries to hold the pen but drops it. He is shaking too much. I say, «Do you want a few strokes?»

He grabs the pen and writes. It's so badly written I can hardly read it. I rewrite it and show him. He nods his head yes. Julie is on a bench behind him. Len knows someone else is with him, I think, but does not know who. I go to the closet and open the safe. There are bundles of cash, hundreds of thousands, and a bundle of papers. Man, what a score this is. The money I'm keeping. I will put it to good use. Shaking with excitement over this score, I go back to Len.

«You've earned a little reprieve with this little score. It's been very expensive putting all those little cameras everywhere. You've made me almost happy. I am going to take your gag off so you can eat and drink. If you say a word, I will lay some more strokes on you. Understand?»

He nods. I go in the kitchen, make a sandwich for him and a glass of water. I take the gag off. He eats, and I put it back on. I go back to his room and stare at the bundle of papers. They seem to be forms with pictures attached. I look at one. A nude girl is posed in a submissive posture. On the back of the picture is written twenty-five thousand dollars. Frowning, I look at the form, and it says what the girl has been trained to do, her obedience level, all sorts of perverted things. It says, «Subject sold in a lot of four.»

I cannot believe this. They are selling girls. What have I stumbled onto? I glance at the other papers. They are the same, only the details are different. The forms even tell the name of the buyer, their contact numbers, even email addresses. The anger I feel is so overwhelming. I have to calm down again before I face Len. I want him to suffer. If I go in there now, I will kill him.

After sitting for a while thinking, I know exactly what to do. I will contact some of the buyers by email with a message. I start to write, telling them Len was caught selling a very large amount of drugs. He was going to inform on you so he would not have to go to prison. Before he could get to the police with the information, we stopped him. He is being held in chains and is undergoing a little behavioural modification.

«Our organization wants to make an example of him. Since you have purchased a large number of girls from us, we have an offer for you. Len has been castrated. We want to give him as a gift to the girls you bought. They may be interested in having him around, a toy to pass the time!»

I am sure they hate Len very much; his punishment will last a very long time. I also tell the buyers, «We would appreciate a quick reply, as some of us want to have him killed. I think he should be made to suffer. Be assured your anonymity will be one of our highest concerns.» I send it off to a few of the buyers on the forms.

I copy the latest Len video to a memory stick and transfer it to my laptop. As I am finishing, I receive an email saying, «Yes, we would love to have this man. Would you let us know when he is ready for transport?» I send a reply saying, «It will be a little while, but he will be transported in the usual way. There will be no charge for this transaction.»

I get a pen and paper, write a list of things I need to know from Len. Number one, who and what were Len's means of transport for the girls? Also, what are his computer password, his email password, and his cell number? Oh, almost forgot the pin number for his bankcard. Of major importance is the name or names of some of the people just as guilty as he is.

I have some immediate plans for Len, but I needed this information first. I go to see Len, making sure Julie cannot hear or see. I don't want to have to kill her. I put the list in front of Len. I free one hand so he can write. He starts to write almost immediately, the writing fairly good this time. When I chain his hand again, I make it a little tighter.

«That was very good. You are turning out to be a very

obedient piece of shit. Was it this easy for you to make the girls give in? Or are you a weak pansy?» I give him a little pat on his ass, the whip making the same satisfying sound. Since the bank is just down the street, I think a quick withdrawal is in order. His limit is five hundred a day, a nice bulge in my pocket. I get back to the apartment. I check the numbers and passwords he gave me. They all work. For now, I will have to trust the delivery instructions. I go back to Len.

«I want to conduct a little experiment. They say testosterone controls aggression and the sex drive. I can see that you suffer from an excess of both. I would like to put that to a test.» I get a mirror and a leather shoelace. I make a loop of the shoelace, snare his balls in it, and pull it as tight as I can. I tie it off and put the mirror in a place he can see them. He looks at me in horror. Am I really going to do this to him?

I smile at him and say, «Enjoy the show, okay? I've already seen one just like it, so I won't bother sticking around. That show was in this very room, and I bet you can guess who the star was? Don't worry; it does not hurt for long. See ya soon.»

I really am enjoying this too much. Maybe I am sick after all? I decide it is probably time to go home. People may be wondering where I am. Frank is waiting for me when I get home. He looks like he's been awake for hours, his eyes all red, and his face blotchy.

«Where have you been? I've been worried about you. Disappearing from the hospital like that, you had people looking all over for you.»

«When I came to, it was the same room I woke up in before. Too many memories. I had to get out. I went to eat, and then my shoulder hurt so much I had to get some painkillers. I left the hospital before I got some.

«More importantly, how are you doing? I'm so sorry for the loss of Margaret. I know exactly how you feel. She was your sister-in-law, too many emotions to deal with,» I say to Frank.

«To be honest, I am only feeling the betrayal right now. It's Amy I feel for. It must be terrible for her,» Frank says. «How are you, Chris, really? I want to know the truth. Do you feel like getting high?»

«You know, that's the farthest thing from my mind,» I answer truthfully, surprising myself.

«We are looking for Julie now. The video from the apartment at your work proves it was her and Mark's drugs. They kept talking about how much money they lost, all sorts of things. They even described the method of getting it in the country, how they would have to find another way of getting it in. It even shows her dad's involvement,» Frank tells me, the only good thing in all this mess.

«The last I heard, Julie was in the hospital,» I lie, straight-faced. «If I see her I'll hold on to her for you. I gotta go lie down, feeling pretty shaky.»

«Okay,» Frank nods. «We will talk soon.» Good. I can get rid of Julie real soon. I have work to do, and it's better if she's taken care of. I go to the police station to check in and see if they need a statement from me. They tell me the prosecutor will look after that in a few weeks. I ask to see if I know any of the girls in lockup, and one of the officers takes me back to the holding area. I see three women I know. I tell them about Julie, what she was doing to young girls, getting them hooked on heroin, making them turn tricks, and even selling them into slavery. All the girls were underage. The police do not know this part yet, but I do, and now so do the girls in jail. I want Julie to suffer, A good friend's niece was one of her victims. There are possibly hundreds of victims.

The girls in the cell assure me that Julie will be well taken care of. Perfect. Another person taken care of. Her torment will really begin when she gets out of jail. I have big plans for her. I go back to Len's to see how he is.

«Hey, Len, how are you doing? How are they hanging?»

I look around the apartment a little more. I want to find some heroin to give Julie. I need her semiconscious again. She used to do heroin sometimes but not for a while. I intend to change that, and it will not take much. I look in Art's room this time and find some, along with another few thousand dollars. I pocket the money. I find a new syringe and a spoon and mix a hit for her. I look her over, see a big vein, and give her the shot.

She starts nodding off. I get her up and take her to her car. I drive to work, nobody there. I walk her upstairs and give her a bit more junk. I phone Frank and tell him I came to work and Julie was there in the apartment unconscious.

«Better bring some Narcan. I think she took an overdose,» I inform him. Narcan is a drug that cancels the effects of certain drugs. The cops come and take her away. I go for breakfast. Julie kindly left me her car keys, so I drive. I have to disappear for a while. I phone Bob, tell him I am going away for a week or two, maybe three. He is reluctant to let me go. I tell him I have to.

«I've been wanting to get high, maybe go to a treatment center. I need time to get myself straight in the head. Too much has happened,» I explain to him. He finally agrees with me. I know it's because I said if I stay I might get high. I go to the supermarket and buy three shopping carts of food, all my favourites. I take them to Len's, my new home for at least three weeks. I phone Frank and ask him to look after my apartment because I am going away for a while. I explain that I have cleared it with Bob. Frank wishes me good luck.

I make some coffee and put the groceries away. Things could be worse—good TV, lots of DVD's, even some music I like. And besides, there's more entertainment in the next room. Four or five days go by. I visit Len a few hours a day. He is not very aggressive anymore. I guess his balls were the cause.

«I have read up on gelding horses. What I did to you will mean less fear of infection. After a while they will just fall off. The area around the thong will actually heal before they do fall. There will hardly be a scar. That's good, right?» I ask, knowing he can't answer.

Another day I tell him, «I have some good news and some bad news for you. I guess you'll want the good news first.» I hardly even look at him. I strip him and throw his clothes in the dumpster. I have a hose hooked up to wash away his stink.

«You have a new home. Isn't that good news? You will soon be leaving here. One of your customers wants to get a new toy for the girls you sold him. A reunion—how nice for you. Now for the bad news I guess. Are you ready? They need a eunuch. That means no balls and no penis. Now that is bad news. Don't worry; it won't hurt for long.» I get another leather shoelace and tie it as close to his body as possible, pulling it as tight as I can. The mirror is still in place. «Okay, see you tomorrow!» I say with a laugh.

In the morning I have the distasteful job of inserting a catheter. He has to be able to pee.

It takes about three weeks for his balls to fall off, another four days for the penis. They were right. There is hardly a scar. I can tell he must admire his new image; he cannot tear his eyes off the mirror.

«I have another guest coming to visit soon. You even know him. You gave me his name,» I inform him.

«Transport for you is tomorrow. The girls are so excited. So are the guards. They all are homosexual, I'm told. The girls' master does not want his girls having sex with someone other than himself. «I know you will live a long time with them. Don't worry. Be happy. I think that's how the song goes. I think I might even miss you, you weak, fucking pansy!»

Excerpt from the *Vancouver Sun*:

A nude man was found wandering aimlessly in the downtown area Thursday morning. He was shaved bald, with the word 'pedophile' written on his forehead.

Police have revealed that his tongue had been removed and that he was very hard of hearing. Police say when he was discovered that a small amount of blood was still running out of his ear. Unconfirmed reports indicate that all of his genitals had been removed.

Witnesses say the man was bumping into things as he walked, his vision clearly impaired. In addition, a pouch was chained around his waist with the word 'evidence' scrawled on it. Also unconfirmed at this point are reports that a videotaped letter was found on a DVD inside the pouch.

Police confirm the man has been charged with sadism, molestation, and torture of young girls. Apparently, a second DVD provided evidence of the man performing these disgusting acts.

A reliable source has also told this paper that

while still unconfirmed, a note was discovered, which read, «The law is afraid to punish these men, but I am not. He will be the first of many to pay the price for such horrendous deeds. That's how I deal with 'weak, f****** pansies.'»

CPSIA information can be obtained at www.ICGtesting.com
Printed in the USA
LVOW10s1920060216

474042LV00001B/1/P